# A SNAKE IN
# THE OLD HUT

# A SNAKE IN
# THE OLD HUT

### SYLVIA SHERRY

JONATHAN CAPE
THIRTY BEDFORD SQUARE
LONDON

FIRST PUBLISHED 1972
© 1972 BY SYLVIA SHERRY

JONATHAN CAPE LTD, 30 BEDFORD SQUARE, LONDON WC1

ISBN 0 224 00673 8

PRINTED AND BOUND IN GREAT BRITAIN
BY RICHARD CLAY (THE CHAUCER PRESS) LTD, BUNGAY, SUFFOLK
PAPER MADE BY JOHN DICKINSON & CO. LTD

*For George and Elmar*

# I

THE big shadows of clouds swept the wide country silently and regularly from horizon to horizon. They swept with a gentle determination over the distant blue mountains and the tiger-coloured plains, where the umbrella thorns and the round, thatched huts crouched close to the earth. They swept over a herd of giraffe fleeing southward down the Great Valley, and over a single lion sunning itself on a grassy hillock, and they darkened for a moment the still surface of a lake. They brought a momentary chill and a reminder that evening was coming to the boy who stood disconsolately with a stick in his hand thinking of the trouble that day had brought him.

His herd of goats contentedly cropped the sparse grass around him, the leader's bell giving out its small, reassuring tinkle, but the boy's eyes were fixed on the dirt track below him where the pale brown carcass of a dead goat lay. And then he looked up into the burning, blue air above him where a vulture already swirled.

That afternoon the goat had strayed on to the track and been knocked down and killed by a passing car. The car was driven by He-who-has-a-red-face, the white man who owned the nearby farm where Mugo's father worked. He was known for his fast driving and for his bad temper, but when he stopped the car and got out to see what he had hit,

Mugo had loped with long strides down the ridge towards him and, his dark eyes fixing the man's face, had asked for money for the dead goat. Mugo's still, thin figure and serious look had given the man a redder face and his temper had burst out:

"*You* let the goat stray—and look at my dented mud-guard!"

Mugo watched the car drive away in a cloud of red dust. Then he climbed the ridge again, and stood wondering whether he should go home and confess or just run off into the bush.

However, the shadow of the cloud and the sudden chill decided him. At night in the bush it would be much colder, and very dangerous. There'd be wild animals, or forest fighters, or police searching for forest fighters. There were so many enemies. It was better, Mugo decided, to go home and confess. And so he stood up, shouting to the goats to move on, and followed them slowly to the village and, had he known it, to even greater danger.

## 2

HIS family's cluster of round, thatched huts looked strangely deserted for that time of day, for there were usually so many things to see to before dark. Mugo, who had been walking slowly anyway, walked more slowly still when he saw this. Perhaps his two sisters had taken themselves off somewhere and the evening meal wouldn't be ready. Perhaps there had been a meeting and all the family had gone to it. Perhaps, and even worse in these very dangerous days when anything could happen, the village had been attacked by the forest fighters, or his family arrested by the police.

But no. It couldn't be. There was the Homeguard talking to the shopkeeper, ignoring Mugo and his herd of goats. And, in their hut, his two sisters, who had returned from their work in the *shamba*, the family garden, were already busy. One of them was cooking and the other was pouring freshly brewed beer into a gourd, But they were both working with an intensity and silence that was quite unusual.

He wouldn't tell them about the goat. It wasn't their business. He would tell his father and take the consequences. After all, he was almost grown up—he was almost thirteen.

"Where's my father?" he asked.

They did not reply at once, and it suddenly struck him that they didn't usually work in that way, without any gossip or jokes. There *must* be something wrong.

"Where's my father?" he repeated.

Mugo's ugly sister did not pause, but, carefully stirring the pot of stew which hung over the fire, she said, "In his hut." And then, seeing Mugo turn to go, added hastily, "I don't think you should go in there. He's talking to grandfather and some of the elders."

Mugo sat down on a stool.

"I've got something to tell him."

"It'll have to wait."

"It's rather important."

"I doubt it."

Again they worked in silence. Mugo felt more and more anxious. Something was wrong. Had they already heard about the goat? Perhaps He-who-has-a-red-face had been to see his father? Were they sitting in judgment on him already in his father's hut?

"What do you want to tell father?" his beautiful sister asked, curiously.

Mugo met her inquiring gaze with his blank one.

"Nothing."

"But you said you had something ... "

"I'm not telling anybody but him."

"Stubborn!"

"He's always stubborn."

"Stubborn and stupid!"

"I'm not stupid!"

"You look stupid!"

"I'll bet it's nothing important he has to tell, anyway."

Silence again.

"Here," said his beautiful sister at last, "take this beer in to father—and don't spill it. Wait," she added, "let me see if the way is clear," and to Mugo's astonishment she went outside and looked round, very mysteriously. Then she beckoned to him. "Nobody about—go on, now."

Mugo walked with careful steps the short distance to his father's hut. Inside—more surprises. There they sat on the floor, his father, his grandfather and two of the village elders, who were his father's relatives, with their beer gourds before them, but in a deep, thoughtful silence. They hardly seemed to notice Mugo as he poured out more beer. Yet his ugly sister had said they were discussing something. Mugo finished pouring the beer and then loitered unobtrusively in the background, hoping to get a chance to tell his father about the goat.

"If he left at night," said his father at last, "he could probably get away without being noticed."

"And then what happens to him?" asked Mugo's grandfather, after a pause. "How long does night last? What happens in daylight?"

There was a heavy sigh of agreement and much shaking of heads.

"After all," said Mugo's father, "it's his own fault he's in this mess. He should have been more careful. Why should *we* have to put matters right for him?"

"Because we are his relatives. We cannot abandon him, no matter how stupid he has been."

Mugo was immediately convinced they were speaking of him. It was obviously to do with the goat. He-who-has-a-red-face must have threatened to get rid of Mugo for causing an accident. Mugo stepped forward, anxious to speak in his own defence, and his father noticed him for the first time.

"Ah, you're back, Mugo. Did the Homeguard see you as you came in?"

Mugo was astounded. He shook his head. No, the Home-guard in his watch-tower, who was supposed to protect the village, had been gossiping with the shopkeeper, and neither had noticed Mugo.

"He is not very alert, that Homeguard, anyway," said his grandfather. "We can be thankful for that."

"So, no one saw him come here, but no one must see him go. Otherwise we are all in trouble."

"But it was only one goat!" exclaimed Mugo in distress. "One goat only! You can't send me away for one goat!"

"Send *you* away?" They all looked at him in some surprise. "Why should we do that?" And then his father raised his hand. "Wait a moment. A boy would rouse less suspicion than a man."

"That is true. And his absence from the village could be more easily explained."

There was another pause, heavy with thought, while reflective glances were cast upon Mugo, who was beginning to tremble with fear at the strange suggestions being made about him. For a few moments he contemplated running away again. Perhaps he could get to his aunt's village over the ridge—she'd always been kind to him, and she might protect him now. Then his father spoke again:

"What I am going to tell you to do, Mugo, is in strictest secrecy. What you are going to see must never be spoken of. Here," he filled a clean gourd with beer, "carry this carefully to the old hut. Do not let anyone see you going there. Give it to the man you will find there." Mugo's eyes searched his father's face for some explanation of this strange order, but his father only dismissed him with a nod.

As he cautiously left the hut, troubled by the air of mystery over his home that night, Mugo heard his grandfather saying, "Although his grandmother had a high opinion of that boy, it was not one that many people shared. I've never heard him say a sensible thing yet. I don't think it would help matters to have *him* involved."

Darkness was falling; the air was cooling. The old, bare tree that stood up black against the sunset from the still waters of the lake was heavy with roosting pelicans; from the island of papyrus further out a fish-eagle rose, heraldic against the fading sky; and the noise of crickets came louder from the grass and the bushes. Mugo looked over the village, with its huts closely hugging the earth and the quiet spires of smoke from the evening fires. The smell of wood-smoke and cooking lay pungently over the village, and there was no one about. Mugo crossed swiftly over the ground towards the old hut—and tripped on a stone and emptied half the beer down the front of his shirt. He breathed in swiftly as the cold liquid chilled him. It was just his luck!

The old hut had not been used for many years, and part of its roof had fallen in, but because of that it was still light enough inside for Mugo to see clearly the figure lying on the ground there. It was a large animal—a strange, still beast with dark, shiny fur. Mugo saw that in one moment, but the next moment, with a speed that astonished him, the animal had leapt up on to its hind legs. Bewildered, Mugo realized that it had a human face and a gun in its hands that was pointed at him, and a human voice that demanded hoarsely,

"Who are you?"

Spilling more beer, Mugo forced himself to speak calmly. "I'm your nephew, Mugo, Uncle Joshua. Here—some beer."

# 3

THE night was so heavy with fear that Mugo felt he would suffocate. It was fear that got Mugo quickly out of the old hut — that and the very strong smell that came from his uncle, a stronger smell than any animal, the smell of the forest fighter. It clung to Mugo's clothes and hair so that he seemed engulfed in it even outside the hut under the inverted and bejewelled bowl of the evening sky.

He didn't linger in the growing darkness. The smoky warmth and dimness of his father's hut, crowded now with the elders of the village, who materialized silently from the night, was comforting. Crouched behind the hunched figures about the fire, he shuddered as he thought of that wild creature in the old hut.

His grandfather, an old man so thin he reminded one of a polished ebony walking-stick, who was generally totally enveloped at this time in the evening in an old army great-coat to keep out the cold, cast his grandson a cynical glance, his head popping out of the coat like the head of a tortoise.

"You remember your uncle Joshua, eh, Mugo?"

Mugo remembered him, though he had changed so much since the first time he had seen him. That would be three years ago. He had come to the village just as suddenly and unexpectedly then as he had now, only then he had not come secretly, but had walked openly into the village among the scattered groups of family huts, a very tall, handsome young man with a smooth, round face, narrow, flat eyes and a wide nose, who walked very straight with his head held high. He had been very earnest and very talkative. He came to talk and he *did* talk, seeking people out in their huts and gathering them together in the open under the old fig tree just beyond the headman's hut. There, standing in the gently shifting shadows of the leaves, thin and upright, with his dark skin shining against his white shirt and a red-and-green cotton scarf round his neck and his head thrown back, he had talked fiery talk to the villagers grouped before him—the elders with their staffs and bunches of ceremonial leaves, the young men eagerly listening, the women, with their smooth-shaven heads and glittering earrings, concerned about their children who squatted on the earth, lost among a forest of black legs.

"How long will you sit under the rule of the white man?" Joshua had cried. "How long will you let him devour the land that belongs to you? Let us drive the white man into the sea! Didn't our prophets foretell years ago that the white men would come? 'If you touch them, the skin will remain in your hand,' they said, 'because it is so soft. And they will destroy us with thunder and fire!' But have they destroyed us?"

"No!" shouted the villagers.

"And will they destroy us?"

"No!" they chanted.

"But they have taken our land and our freedom. We want back land and freedom!"

"Land and freedom!"

"And Ngai, Almighty God, has willed that it shall be so. Listen to me, for you are like goats and sheep grazing with

15

your heads to the ground, but I am like a giraffe with a long neck so that I can see—a long way into the future! I tell you, the tree of freedom is planted, but if it is to grow it will need a lot of watering with human blood." Raising a clenched fist against the high, blue sky, he had shouted, "The land will run with blood and echo with the shrieks of the tortured, but out of it will come freedom!"

Mugo, younger then, had been frightened by these words, and he had heard his father and grandfather muttering, "Such fiery talk—this will bring trouble." But a great murmur of approval, like the roar of a distant storm, had come from the villagers.

"Ngai has willed it!" they shouted. "It is time we took our country back from the white man!"

That had been the beginning, Mugo knew. Joshua did not come back, but soon afterwards, two young men from the village had left to go to the capital and join Joshua and his friends. Rumours swept through the village at intervals, brought by a passing merchant or the women back from market. The white men were arresting all people who spoke as Joshua had spoken. "What news of Joshua?" people asked. "What has happened to Joshua?" Then came the reply—"He has gone with many others into the forests on the mountains. He has gone to join the forest fighters." And trouble really started for the ordinary people. The forest fighters had a habit of suddenly descending on villages and police posts to get guns and ammunition and food and supporters—and sometimes to kill those they thought had betrayed them to the white man. The government put a watch-tower in each village with homeguards to guard the villages. It was not a happy time for anyone, but especially if you had a relation in the forest the government kept its many eyes upon you. And so Mugo and his family were under constant suspicion, and the Homeguard was particularly inclined to insist on searching their huts on the slightest pretext.

But there was little resemblance between the young man who made that fiery speech and the strange creature in the hut, clothed in animal skins, its long hair twisted into numerous thin plaits. The flat, narrow eyes had been as restlessly alert as a nervous monkey's, the nostrils twitched like the nostrils of a stray dog. He was a wary animal, listening for danger. Mugo had nothing to say to this fierce stranger who had a bloody bandage wrapped round one leg and another tied over a wounded eye.

Only one thing was the same, Mugo thought. Joshua brought fear with him before, and he brought fear with him again.


"It seems to be true," Mugo's father was saying, flinging down on to the floor in the centre of the group a thin stick about a foot long, "it seems to be true that my brother Joshua has quarrelled with his leader in the forest, the famous general called Mwengo. It seems to be true," and here he threw another stick, "that Mwengo accused Joshua of trying to kill him, and drew a gun and shot Joshua twice."

"Noguo, noguo—that's it, that's it," everyone agreed, and one of the elders picked up the two sticks and again threw them down saying, "But how are we to know the truth of what has happened in the forest? How are we to know the truth about this quarrel between Joshua and Mwengo?"

And Mugo's father flung a stick down impatiently.

"The truth or untruth does not matter. Only two things matter." He threw another stick. "Joshua has come to his relatives for protection and help." Another stick. "His relatives should do all they can for him."

"Noguo! Noguo!" The murmur ran round the shadowy hut.

Here, Mugo's grandfather took up the sticks and added them to a bundle of such sticks he had in his hand, and everybody knew they were in for a long talk. When serious matters were discussed in the village, the sticks were always used. Each stick represented one point being made, and the man with the sticks could not be interrupted till he had made his point.

"So Joshua has an enemy in the forest—the leader Mwengo, who will surely come hunting him. And if Mwengo learns that we have helped Joshua, he will have *us* murdered."

"Noguo, noguo!"

"Do you understand also, though, that the danger does not only come from Mwengo, but from the other side? The police,"—down went a stick—"the army,"—another stick—"the homeguard,"—another stick—"they will all be seeking Joshua once they know he has left the forest, and they will all be after us if they know we have sheltered him."

"Noguo, noguo!"

The loud murmur of agreement filled the dim and crowded hut, and as the men talked, throwing suggestions and warnings back and forward, a plan took shape.

The men agreed that Joshua must leave. He must be got away so that the village would be safe and Joshua would be safe. He would have to travel the many hundreds of miles down to the coast, to Mombasa, the only place where he could get on a ship, an Arab dhow, to take him to Egypt and to safety. True, it would be a dangerous and difficult journey, for he would be hunted both by Mwengo and by the police; true, he would be without any official papers of identification; and true, he would be, once in Egypt, for ever a stranger, an outcast from his own country. But was this was not better than death? Another stick was thrown.

"Noguo, noguo," the men nodded. They drank more beer. Certainly it was the only solution.

There was another pause, a longer one, expressing their satisfaction at having reached this conclusion. Mugo left the hut. It seemed to him also that everything was under control, everything in the hands of the elders. They would see that Joshua went away.

Much later, he was wakened out of a deep sleep by a hand on his shoulder. In the now empty hut, only the lingering smell of beer and snuff, the bright glow from the embers of the fire, remained of the meeting of elders.

"Mugo—"

Sleepily Mugo grunted, and his father spoke quietly out of the darkness.

"You heard the elders' plan for Joshua?"

"He's going to Mombasa."

"But how is he to go?"

Mugo's eyes closed sleepily. He could not understand why his father had wakened him.

"Mugo, listen—he is wounded. How can a wounded man travel so far? He must hide his wounded eye with dark glasses and pretend to be blind. He must carry a long stick and pretend to be lame."

Mugo sat up, suddenly wide awake. He had a vision of Joshua, blind and lame, limping his way through the country to Mombasa. There was something wrong with the vision. Something missing.

"He must have a guide," he said.

"Yes, Mugo—a guide. A boy leading a blind and lame relative would attract very little attention ... "

"A boy ... " Mugo was silent as understanding came to him.

Early next morning Mugo sat outside his sisters' hut with an untasted bowl of corn and vegetable stew in his hand, looking reflectively over the great lake moving sluggishly under the brilliant gaze of the sun. He did not look in the direction of the old hut. His mind had been restless all night with dreams of Joshua and the long journey his father wanted him to take. It seemed incredible to Mugo. It could not be true, he thought. He must have imagined the plan. His father could not send him on such a journey.

But then his father's quiet voice came back to him: "You know the danger we are in from Joshua. All of us. You must go on this long and dangerous journey for the sake of the family, for the sake of Joshua, who is a relative. In any case, it is the decision of the village."

And finally, those last words: "Your grandmother thought you would be a great leader. Are you ready to prove her right?"

"No," Mugo protested to himself. "No. Not yet!"

He thought of his grandmother, that very old woman, in her smoke-filled hut, watching him and two of his friends eating roasted maize-cob around her fire. She had never given any sign until just before her death that she thought highly of Mugo.

But when she had stood in the crowd listening to Joshua's speech that day, Mugo had seen her shaking her head and drawing her lips together and muttering, "There can be no good in him. He is Njangu come back. His face is the face of Njangu. And Njangu had the evil in his blood."

Mugo had stared up into her small, still face as she looked sideways at Joshua as though unwilling to look directly into his face, and he had wondered. And later he had gone into her smoky hut, his eyes stinging and watering as they always did when he entered it, and had asked her who Njangu was. His grandmother's smooth-shaved head was bent, gleaming through the steam from the cooking-pot on the fire, and she had looked at Mugo from the corners of her eyes and shaken her head again.

"Njangu was our ancestor. My great-grandfather told me about him so that he would not be forgotten and so that the family would always be on guard against his evil."

"How was he evil?"

"He was a wicked boy and a wicked man. He was only seven when he killed three goats in the herd he was looking after. But people said he was young, and they excused him. Then he tied his young brother to a tree and left him in the sun, and he died. But people said he was only thoughtless. He injured other boys—he beat them with sticks till the blood ran, and he dug a trap and a boy fell in it and starved to death—Oi! Oi! Such evil! He was called Njangu by his friends, that means rough and treacherous. And rough and treacherous he was."

"What happened to him?"

"At last, when our people said it must end, he was driven

21

from the village. What happened to him then, whether the hyenas or the wild dogs ate him, or the spirits entered his body, nobody knew. Nobody cared. But his evil stayed in the blood of the family, and sometimes it comes out again in somebody—somebody like Joshua."

"But grandmother," said Mugo, "people say Joshua is a *hero*."

"Joshua is also Njangu!" retorted his grandmother. "He has the evil in his blood."

Her words echoed again in Mugo's mind, and he thought of that strange animal-like figure in the old hut. Wasn't it rumoured of Joshua that in battle he wiped the blood of his first victim from his knife and placed it in his mouth saying, "The blood of an enemy is sweet"? It couldn't be true that he was to go on a long and dangerous journey with this descendant of Njangu!

The village went about its concerns as usual that morning, and in his family's compound his sisters were tidying up, and serving breakfast. His grandfather, still in his greatcoat, shuffled over to eat a bowl of stew noisily and with great relish, seemingly unaware of Mugo's predicament. But he knew, everybody in the village knew, what had been planned. Only the Homeguard knew nothing about it.

And now, from the direction of the tower, they saw the Homeguard ambling towards them, the sunlight glinting on his rifle.

"I'll be missed from the village," Mugo protested suddenly and desperately. "I'll be missed and *he*"—nodding towards the Homeguard—"will be immediately suspicious."

But his beautiful sister only laughed and said, "Missed? You? Just wait and see!"

And his grandfather, shrugging himself further into his coat, murmured, "Whatever his grandmother said about him, I don't think that boy could lead a donkey to Mombasa!"

# 4

THE Homeguard was wearing a heavy pair of old boots and the right boot had split open at the toe. The two boots were planted astride on the ground just in front of Mugo, and above them rose a pair of wrinkled socks and then the dark brown legs with the scar across the left shin where, so the story went, his first wife had bitten him in a fit of rage when he had come home drunk one evening many years before. The Homeguard's version of the story was, however, that the scar had been left by a snake-bite. Above his knees were his khaki shorts, pressed into knife-like creases, and then his well-ironed shirt. The Homeguard had a long narrow nose, and a permanently superior expression. He was fond of telling anyone who would listen of how he hobnobbed with He-who-has-a-red-face and with Chief Inspector Mackenzie, and he really thought of himself as a white man. The white man who fell into the black sea, the village boys used to call him, and often imitated his strutting walk about the village, sternly telling each other, "Do your duty diligently *and* scientifically," which was a favourite saying of his.

"I have come", he said, "to commiserate with you. I have heard a rumour that your relative Joshua is at present being hunted over the country."

Mugo's beautiful sister laughed loudly and scornfully.

"You think that troubles us? Are we being hunted? And are *you* one of the hunters?"

The Homeguard tried to ignore this, as coming from a woman, but at the same time he was very much attracted to Mugo's beautiful sister and did not want to offend her.

"I'm sorry, but in the course of duty I must search your huts. This is not my idea. My instructions come from *Higher Up*."

The two sisters giggled. "Higher up? How high?" they asked, and looked up at the sky. And the ugly sister observed the vulture. "What is that vulture doing? What is dead there?" she asked, but the Homeguard had never taken much notice of her.

"You won't mind if I begin here?" asked the Homeguard.

"No, no. Come in. Come in. After all, we do not expect privacy any longer. Especially when we have the friend of important people living in the village," said Mugo's beautiful sister sarcastically. "Come in, come in. Look, this is our grinding-stone—here are our beds—empty, you see. We are only two sisters living together. What more would you expect. No, no. Don't hesitate. Search everywhere, turn everything upside down!"

Mugo and his father said nothing. Sitting there, they anxiously watched the Homeguard, waiting for the moment when he would turn his attention to the old hut. But Mugo's beautiful sister was really upsetting the man. He was growing clumsy and embarrassed, and besides he was troubled that this girl was getting angry at him. After all, she was the most beautiful girl in the village, and he had been hoping to get together enough goats to allow him to buy her as a wife. Still, he had his duty to do, and having searched one hut, he turned away to the next.

"He will find Joshua," murmured Mugo's father. The family remained together while the sun grew warmer, the fire crackled, the goats bleated and the vulture hung in the sky above, and they watched without speaking while the Homeguard disappeared into the other hut. They could hear various thumps and clatterings as he moved about. And Mugo distinctly saw the dark, animal-like figure of his uncle for just a moment at the door of the old hut before he disappeared again. Joshua must have seen the Homeguard arrive. What would he do? Would he shoot the Homeguard if he came near? That would certainly bring disaster on them.

The Homeguard came out of the men's hut, and began to walk towards the old hut. He went slowly but firmly, his boots stirring up the dust at every step.

Suddenly Mugo stood up, for the first time inspired to do something.

"Homeguard!" he shouted. "Be careful!"

Mugo's father gripped his arm warningly. The Homeguard turned.

"What's the matter?"

"Be careful! There's a snake in the old hut."

The Homeguard hesitated, suspicious.

"It was there yesterday—it bit a goat that went in and the goat—the goat died."

"Why did you not kill the snake?"

"It was too dark. Perhaps it's gone now."

Still the Homeguard looked suspicious.

"If you see it in there, you could kill it for us—shoot it with your rifle … "

The Homeguard came towards them. "Do you think the government pays me to go around shooting snakes in old huts for you? Do you think my time is not more valuable than that?"

Mugo began to breathe more easily. His face was without expression as he looked at the Homeguard. "Well, but we have no guns for killing snakes, and so I thought you might kill it for us."

"Be quiet, Mugo," interrupted his father, who was also beginning to relax a little. "Do not trouble such a busy man."

The Homeguard, rather relieved that he had not had to arrest a dangerous forest fighter, stood before them, with his right boot gaping thirstily. "It is not so much the trouble," he explained, smiling, "as the wasting of ammunition, you understand. Of government ammunition.

"Please, please," he went on, hastily, "don't think I suspect you, or that I intend to carry out my orders. Not where friends are concerned. Why, I know that you would immediately tell me if any forest fighter came this way."

"Oh," said Mugo's beautiful sister, giving him a beautiful smile, "do you really trust us?"

And the Homeguard smiled also, and nodded, and went away again, feeling that he might yet marry the beautiful sister.

"We must get Joshua out of here," said Mugo's father between clenched teeth, wiping sweat from his brow. "Otherwise we are all in prison."

For a while the family sat outside the hut pretending to eat a breakfast they had no appetite for; only the old grandfather went on eating. They cast anxious glances towards the old hut, expecting to see Joshua's strange, wild figure appear but nothing moved in the shadows there.

Mugo's father spoke in a low, earnest tone. "You must

go with Joshua to Mombasa. You must get him away from the village and out of the country. Then he will never trouble us again. You must go with him, Mugo, to be part of his disguise and to make sure that we are rid of him."

There was a silence among the five of them, as they thought their own thoughts about this. Mugo's sisters felt sure he could never see such a dangerous journey through. Mugo was only frozen into an enormous fear of that man who had the evil in his blood and of the long journey ahead.

Then his dark eyes, that moved like drops of water beneath his lashes, caught sight of the vulture hovering in the sky, and he remembered that he had yet to confess about the goat!

Mugo's ugly sister was staring upwards again.

"What's that vulture after?" she asked.

Mugo made up his mind.

"I will go with Uncle Joshua to Mombasa." It was, anyway, the only way he could see of avoiding trouble over the goat.

"My son," said his father, "I always knew your grandmother was right about you. Already you have shown your cunning by tricking the Homeguard, and now you show courage by offering to go with your uncle."

"Leadership! Courage!" muttered his grandfather. "This is the boy who cannot take a herd of goats grazing without getting one of them killed!"

Mugo's dark eyes glistened under his lashes as he stared at his grandfather. How long had he known about the goat?

His father smiled. "We'll say no more about that."

# 5

THEY made no secret of Mugo's journey for the next day. It was the reason for the family's change of routine; for his sisters' not going to work in the *shamba*. Mugo's ugly sister was busily preparing food for his journey, and making swift and secret trips to the old hut to help Joshua prepare also. She came back once carrying the reddish-brown, bush-buck skin jacket that Joshua said he had not taken off since the skin dried round his body. She could not burn it, yet the coat and its smell had to be got rid of, and so she buried it behind the hut.

And later that morning, Mugo was marched ostentatiously by his beautiful sister to the village store.

"What can one do with this boy?" she asked loudly of all the women there. "Here he is to go on a visit to his aunt, and he will need a new pair of shoes. His others are worn in holes—and he has had them only one year! The expense!"

There was a great deal of sympathetic clucking from the women, and Mugo stood completely unhappy among the curry powders, the sacks of mealies and the tins of paraffin.

"Ha! Those will do, those will do!" exclaimed his beautiful sister, as Mugo stumped up and down the store in a new pair of shoes. "Doesn't matter if they're a size too big. He also grows very fast."

"*One* size too big! These shoes are like boats!" complained Mugo, but nobody took any notice of that.

Then he saw the Homeguard at the entrance to the shop, curious about all this.

"If he is walking over the ridge to see his aunt, he won't need new shoes. He'll be better in bare feet," the Homeguard said.

"So! You know all about it, I suppose! Who said it was his aunt over the ridge? It is his aunt in Nairobi. Surely you know he will need shoes in Nairobi? Just for sitting in! Nobody is expecting him to *walk* in them!"

However, although his beautiful sister was so quick, Mugo was at once an object of suspicion to the Homeguard.

"Perhaps," he said softly, and slyly, to Mugo, "your aunt may have news of your uncle Joshua."

Mugo stood quite still and fixed his dark stare on the Homeguard's face.

"Your aunt, now," he went on, "that will be She-with-the-gap-between-her-teeth?"

"No, it will not!" interrupted Mugo's beautiful sister, tartly. "That is his aunt who lives over the ridge. His aunt who lives in Nairobi is She-who-has-bow-legs. And she is a very successful woman. She looks after the children of a European and she has a hut in the middle of his garden all to herself and surrounded by grass and frangipani trees."

"I very much doubt that!" said the Homeguard.

"Are you calling me a liar?" shrieked Mugo's beautiful sister.

The Homeguard stared at her for a long time and then departed without another word.

"Tonight, after dark, I will guide you to the road and leave you near the place where the bus stops." The voice was an urgent whisper in the dimness of the old hut where Mugo, his father and his uncle Joshua sat. "You will have to hide there, and Mugo will meet you in the morning. You will both get the bus to Nakuru."

It was not yet quite dark, so that inside the hut Mugo could make out the occasional movement of his father's hand and the gleam of his uncle's white shirt front, and the red earth just inside the doorway still glowed in the last rays of the sun. As he spoke, Mugo's father traced marks in that patch of earth with a stick, making, with deep furrows, a map of the journey they were to take. There was the big circle representing their village and a line leading to the bus stop which was just a dot, and now the stick traced a wavering line for the road to Nakuru. Nakuru, Mugo noticed, was a smaller circle than their village, and he concluded it must be just a smaller village. He concentrated as hard as he could on memorizing the map and everything his father said.

"At Nakuru, you will get the train to Nairobi," the stick made another curving line and stopped with another small circle. Yet, thought Mugo, I was always told that Nairobi was a big town.

When his father stopped speaking, Mugo could hear only the heavy sound of his uncle's breathing.

"It is putting the boy in great danger." Mugo was surprised that Joshua's voice was not so hoarse as it had been. It seemed that when he had washed in the water the ugly sister had taken him, and cut his hair and taken off his animal skins and put on the trousers and shirt and long over-coat that had been given to him he had changed his voice as well. But still, Mugo knew, his eyes rolled, and his nostrils flared, and he was always on the alert.

"Mugo will take that risk. He is no coward."

Mugo could not repress a shiver. He had never travelled on a bus before and he had never seen a train, the iron snake that spits fire, as the old men of the village called it. He was afraid of such monsters.

His father's voice went on. "At Nairobi, Mugo, you will seek out your aunt, She-who-has-bow-legs, at the house of the white man, He-who-whistles. Your aunt will see that you get on the train at Nairobi that will take you"—again the stick traced its line—"to Mombasa." Another circle. "And Mombasa is on the edge of the sea." Here there was much stirring up of the ground beside the last circle.

"What is that?" whispered Mugo.

"That is the sea, boy. Did I not say so?"

"The sea is earth stirred up?"

"The sea is water."

Mugo had never seen the sea either.

"Many years ago," went on his father, "I was in Mombasa and I worked for Sheikh Ali Mohammed in his warehouse in the Old Town. Now the Old Town is a very confusing place to a stranger, but you will find his warehouse just off Salim Road, behind the Jain Temple. Remember that, Mugo. Sheikh Ali Mohammed will not have forgotten me. He will get Joshua on to a ship—this I do know."

Joshua spoke quietly out of the darkness.

"I could stay here till my wounds heal. Then I would return to the forest."

"And what about Mwengo?"

"I would *kill* Mwengo!" Joshua snarled, and his gun

flashed suddenly in his hand. "The Decider here would settle him."

Mugo's father ignored the gun. "You cannot stay here. It is too dangerous—for all of us."

"So, you will not risk a little danger for the man who risked everything for your freedom?" scoffed Joshua.

"If you thought so much of your people then, you wouldn't endanger them now!"

"Such gratitude!" The whispering voices ceased, and the loud noise of crickets filled the hut. Mugo stirred uneasily on the cold earth floor.

"I'll go. Tomorrow. But I go alone."

"You cannot stay and you cannot go alone. It is the village's decision. We must abide by it. The boy goes with you."

"He is not needed! Do you think I—Joshua—need to rely on a boy?"

"You need to obey the family's decision!"

The angry hissing of their voices rose and fell, and Mugo ventured at last, "I don't mind staying."

"You are going with him. There is a need for you to make this journey. You understand this, Mugo!"

Mugo said no more. He understood only too well.

"And you understand *this*?" Joshua's voice was low and threatening. "If the boy comes with me, he comes at his own risk. I have no time to watch over him. If it is necessary, if it is dangerous for *me* to keep him, I will abandon him. Wherever we might be!"

Mugo's father did not seem to be moved. "You will be glad the boy is with you. And you cannot abandon your kinsman. I entrust him to you."

There was only a low growl from Joshua, the growl of a

c

creature in a trap, but if that worried Mugo, it did not seem to worry his father.

"Nothing can go wrong with the plan," he murmured, more lightly. "See, here is the map as plain as the path through the village. Nothing can go wrong," and he smoothed over the red earth, obliterating the map and patting the earth smooth.

"For a start," whispered Joshua, "that is wrong. Do you want to rouse suspicions? Why should that patch of earth at the entrance to an old hut be patted smooth? Roll your stick over it, make it look like all the rest of the earth."

His father's hand, after a pause, rolled the stick slowly over the earth, as Joshua suggested.

"There is one more thing," Mugo's father insisted. "You must leave your gun here."

Joshua did not reply, but Mugo felt him stiffening in the darkness.

"Almost certainly a gun of that size would be noticed by someone as you were travelling."

"I go nowhere without the Decider."

"If the police find it on you—say in Nairobi—you would have no defence. You must leave it."

"It is stained with the blood of my enemies. It goes with me."

"Then let the boy carry it. No one will search him for weapons."

Joshua was silent for a time, then he said quietly, out of the darkness, "Let him take it. And let him take good care of it until I need it again." Joshua went on in a low, determined voice. "And understand this. Since you will not let me stay till my wounds heal, I'll take the boy with me to avoid suspicion. I'll keep him with me and follow your plan as

34

long as it's safe for me. After that—the responsibility is not mine!"

Mugo's father grunted. "You were always a big talker, Joshua." He stood up. "It's time for us to go. My eldest daughter will give you food, and Mugo will have money with him for the journey. Come."

"You do not trust *me* with the money? Is that what you mean?"

"Does anyone trust the wounded lion?"

"Wait!" Joshua raised his voice. "Someone's coming."

They stood listening—there was no sound but the crickets.

"No one is coming," said Mugo's father.

"Someone is coming!" Joshua was so commanding that they both obeyed him, standing silently, and sure enough, after a while, they heard a voice in the distance, coming closer. It was only an old man of the village returning drunk and singing aloud to himself in the night. He passed close by the hut and then his voice faded.

"Now," said Joshua, "now we can go."

"The boots—better put them on." Mugo's father handed a pair to Joshua.

"Bootmarks along your village paths—wouldn't that make people suspicious?" he whispered scornfully. "I'll carry them."

Left alone in the darkness of the old hut, Mugo listened till the shuffling of their footsteps had faded. He wondered whether he should, even at this late date, risk the dangers of the night and flee over the ridge to his aunt. Buses, trains, strange towns, the sea, the forest fighters, the police—and Uncle *Joshua*.

"I must be brave," he said to himself. And then, cautiously, he stretched out his hand and his fingers gripped the butt of the gun. He drew it to him, bending to look at it in the vanishing light. Then he went very quickly to where the firelight glowed through the doorway of his sisters' hut.

"Here, Mugo," said his beautiful sister from where she was wrapping up a bundle on the floor. "Here—come and see what I am packing for you. Look, a clean shirt, a clean pair of trousers, your new shoes, some roast meat wrapped up in palm leaves and some sweet potatoes. Now all of these I am wrapping up in a blanket to make a neat bundle for you. You will probably feel cold travelling in the train and the blanket will be useful."

"And here, Mugo," said his father later, "here is the money for the journey. Put it carefully in your trouser pocket and do not lose it. Without it you are helpless!"

Before he slept that night, Mugo pushed the Decider down to the bottom of his bundle, under the food and his clothes, and kept the bundle at his side all night.

People in the village, in those days, did not make a long journey casually and unnoticed, and when Mugo started off early next day to walk to the road where he would catch the bus for Nakuru, most of the villagers were there to watch him go, and the boys formed a singing group to go with him part of the way and sing songs to put heart into him.

> Mugo starts his long journey—
> Woee!
> Did his grandmother not proclaim him great?
> Woee!
> When shall we see Mugo again?
> When he returns from the great city!
> Who knows how great he will be then?
> Woee! Woee!

they sang, dancing along behind Mugo who trudged forward, the red earth churning over his bare feet, and the Homeguard watched suspiciously from the tower.

"Only you know, my friends," sang Mugo at the verge of the village, "what this journey means to me!"

"Only Ngai knows", they sang, "whether he will return! Go well, Mugo!"

"Stay well, friends!"

# 6

IT took all Mugo's courage to keep on walking towards the
bus stop where he was to meet that most feared and peculiar
man who was his uncle Joshua and begin this very dangerous
journey into the unknown. Over four hundred miles — he
couldn't begin to imagine such a distance!

Many times he stopped on the narrow path to the road to
look back to the point over the ridge where he knew his
village was and where he could still see the lake glossy in
the morning sunlight. But again and again he would pick up
his bundle, its heaviness reminding him of the Decider, and
walk on. Occasionally, when he heard a distant goat-bell
ringing clearly, his heart would turn over in his breast and
settle heavy inside him.

His thoughts were interrupted by something he noticed
suddenly in the red earth of the path before him — something which puzzled him very much — the marks of a man's
shoes. They stretched on ahead of him along the path.
Mugo stopped and looked back. As far as he could see he
could trace the imprint of those shoes. He found that very
curious, because nobody in the area would have been likely
to wear shoes on that path, but they looked very like the
shoes his father had given to Joshua and which he had carefully not worn in the village so as to avoid arousing suspicion. Yet if the Homeguard saw these footprints he would

be *very* suspicious. His uncle Joshua *couldn't* suddenly have become careless?

Mugo stood in the deep, warm silence, puzzling over this problem, his eyes still tracing the marks of those footprints back to the village. And suddenly he started. Surely that had been a man's face peering out of that distant bush at him? Mugo stared hard at the bush, but he could see no face now. He must have been mistaken. He walked on again, but he had an uneasy feeling that he was being followed. Now and then he would stop suddenly and turn, hoping to surprise anyone who was following him; and once he saw the branches of a bush shaking wildly, and once he thought he saw the glint of a rifle among the long grass.

It took Mugo a good hour to reach the road, and the shoe-prints went all the way, and so did the uneasy feeling of being followed. It was a narrow road of rough, red earth pitted with pot-holes and bordered by trees and bushes and grass that had a film of red dust over them, for it had been a very dry season and everything was dusty and waiting for the rains. Mugo knew the bus would stop there for them—his father had said so—but the thought of getting inside that clumsily moving and noisy animal and trusting himself to it did nothing to lighten his heart.

And there was no sign of his uncle, and the grass verge did not reveal footprints. Mugo looked up and down the road, but Joshua was not there. For a moment, his heart felt lighter. Perhaps his uncle had changed his plans and gone off on his own. If he did not appear before the bus came, Mugo decided, he would return home, and his troubles would be over. He put his bundle on the ground and watched the flight of a bird over the far blue sky.

He had heard nothing, and yet he turned quickly, sensing

a presence. Beside him, as though he had always been there, stood a silent, very still figure, leaning on a long staff, a man in old trousers and shirt and a long coat, with dark glasses concealing his eyes. He stood listening.

"I didn't hear you coming!"

Joshua gave no sign. He did not even look at Mugo. Mugo traced a line in the dusty road with his big toe, and noticed that his uncle was wearing shoes, but he hadn't the courage to remark on this. Rough and treacherous. He could not get his grandmother's words out of his mind. Mugo glanced quickly at Joshua, but he seemed withdrawn into himself, unaware of his nephew.

"Your father gave you some money?" Joshua's hand was stretched out towards him suddenly, the blank gaze of the glasses turned on him.

Mugo hesitated. "He said *I* should carry it because a blind man might easily be robbed."

"How much?"

"A great deal. Twenty-five shillings."

Joshua grinned derisively. "Is that supposed to get us to Mombasa? Four hundred miles to Mombasa?"

"Surely it will?" It seemed a lot of money to Mugo.

"It will cost at least fifteen shillings to get us to Nairobi."

Mugo was astonished. So much? One would have to be very rich to travel far. And how could they now get to Mombasa? Perhaps they should put the journey off ...

"Is this the money?" Joshua, the blind man, stooped to pick up a small packet that lay on the red earth at Mugo's feet. Mugo took the money from him and put it into the pocket of his shirt. It was his beautiful sister's fault. He had asked her to sew up the hole in his trouser pocket, and she hadn't done it. His uncle's scorn made him feel stupid, and that his family was stupid also. Mugo stared ahead un-comfortably, then he burst out, "Anyway, if you're sup-posed to be blind, how did you see the money on the ground?"

"It's as well I did."

There was an unfriendly silence, and then Joshua grasped his arm.

"We're being watched—no, don't look round!"

Mugo longed to turn round. Joshua must have eyes in the back of his head.

"I heard a twig snap—and I feel there's someone there. They've followed you from the village. Why weren't you more careful?"

Angry again with himself, Mugo remembered the sus-picions he'd had. He ought to have taken more notice of them, he realized that now. Suppose whoever it was tried to arrest Joshua?

"Did anyone see you leave the village?"

Joshua's blank gaze over the countryside made Mugo increasingly uneasy.

"Everybody."

"You mean—*everybody* saw you leave?"

"That was my father's plan."

"Plan!" Joshua sneered. "A plan for disaster."

"It's a good plan," Mugo protested. "And in two days we will be in Mombasa. In any case, everybody knew you were in the village. They won't tell, though. Only the Home-guard didn't know. I think he followed me."

"That hyena!"

Joshua leaned more heavily on his stick and turned the blank glare of his glasses on Mugo. "The bus is coming."

Mugo could hear nothing, but he was prepared now to take Joshua's word for it. Joshua could obviously see and hear things that nobody else could.

Mugo glanced quickly behind him. "I can't see anybody watching us," he said.

"Do you expect them to stand up and wave to you?" asked Joshua sarcastically.

"It *must* be the Homeguard. Will he try to arrest you?" Joshua only sneered, and Mugo went on quickly, "He's a friend of He-who-has-a-red-face, and he also talks frequently with Chief Inspector Mackenzie." Still Joshua was unimpressed. "I should think", said Mugo anxiously, "he will go and speak about us to Chief Inspector Mackenzie. Sometimes he takes the Chief Inspector presents—chickens and things."

"If he is suspicious, he will phone the police post on the road to look out for us."

Joshua sounded so certain—Mugo began to hate him, but he didn't doubt he was right. It looked as though they were caught before they began.

"Anyway," he said, suddenly angry, "why did you wear shoes? You left a track all the way from the village that the stupidest man could follow."

"You noticed that?" Joshua paused thoughtfully, then shrugged. "It doesn't matter."

There was a low rumbling sound in the distance. Mugo started nervously. His uncle had been right.

"Maybe we shouldn't get on the bus,' he suggested.

He longed to discuss the dangers with his uncle, hoping that with his experience he might be able to reassure him that nothing serious would happen, but he didn't know his uncle at all, and he felt shy about talking to him. So he stood

42

silently, looking back in the direction where his village lay peacefully out of sight over the ridge.

The bus came round the corner like a charging rhino and stopped with a jerk, its hot, angry breath surrounding them.

"Come on," said Joshua and, reluctantly, Mugo moved towards it. "No—wait—you must help me!"

Mugo helped his uncle up the steps and, as he nervously stepped into the bus himself, he caught a glimpse of the Homeguard appearing suddenly on the roadway from the narrow path from the village.


The bus gave a lurch that threw Mugo forward, and he clutched the seat in front of him desperately. They were moving, and the movement made him feel dizzy. But then, when he looked out of the window he had a strange feeling that they weren't moving, but that the trees and fields of vegetables outside were moving in the opposite direction and at great speed. Mugo felt his head spinning. "Ooi!" he exclaimed.

"Boy!" hissed his uncle. "Do you want everybody looking at us? Sit back. Control yourself. Where's your courage?"

That brought Mugo up sharp. Nobody would question his courage! He sat back and tried to control his fear, gazing at the back of the seat in front of him instead of out of the window. At least the seat didn't seem to be moving. He succeeded so well that when the conductor came to collect their fares—an event his father had warned him about—he was able to give him the two shillings he asked for and take the ticket quite as though he did it every day of his life.

43

Though two shillings for two pieces of paper seemed to him a terrible waste.

He was about to remark to his uncle that they now had only twenty-three shillings left, when his uncle murmured, looking with his blind gaze straight in front of him,

"There is a police post three miles ahead. If the Home-guard has warned them, they will probably check the passengers in the bus there."

Mugo glanced at his impassive face and dark glasses. Did nothing worry him?

"Are you not afraid?" he asked.

His uncle's lips scarcely moved as he answered, but he sounded ironic as he said, "Of course."


The police post was a neat wooden building painted white with jacaranda trees laden with purple blossom before it, and a policeman on guard at the front door. The bus slowed up and stopped just before the building, so that Mugo could clearly see, inside, in the dimness of the interior, another policeman seated at a desk who watched casually as the bus pulled up.

"They are going to give us up!" he said to his uncle.

"Sit still and say nothing!"

As they watched, the policeman on guard walked down the steps and over to the bus. The conductor got out and the two of them stood together talking. The bus rumbled and shuddered. There was an uneasy silence among its pas-sengers, who in those days always expected trouble, except for the crying of a child and the clucking of a hen from a covered basket.

"Ooi!" exclaimed a woman sitting at the front and overburdened by a huge basket of vegetables she was taking to market. "How long are they going to talk?"

The driver shrugged. He whistled softly to himself as he waited. The policeman at last mounted the steps of the bus and came inside. Sternly he looked round the passengers, his eyes seeming to search each face. His gaze hesitated when it reached Mugo and Joshua, moving from the blind man to the boy curiously. Mugo looked away. He was so tense that his fingers gripped the bundle on his knee like a vice. Yet it seemed to him that Joshua was not at all uneasy.

"Boy," said the policeman in a deep voice.

Mugo started.

"Are you travelling with this blind man?"

"He's my uncle."

Much to Mugo's surprise the policeman said no more. He did not ask to see their papers. He simply nodded, as though that was what he had expected, and then Joshua's voice came clearly through the muted rumble of the engine.

"Why are we waiting here, nephew? Has something happened to the bus?"

In the silence that followed, Mugo felt he must answer just to appear natural.

"No—no, uncle. Just a police check."

His voice seemed very squeaky to him, but the policeman took no notice. He left the bus, the engine revved, the conductor jumped on board.

"We're safe!" whispered Mugo.

## 7

MUGO sat back with a sigh. He closed his eyes, and in a moment he relaxed in the warmth of the sun, the cooling draught of air through the glassless windows, the soothing movement of the bus. He opened his eyes and found he was no longer dizzy looking out and could begin to appreciate the heavy woodland, the fields of grain, the sleek cattle they passed.

He glanced surreptitiously at his uncle, at the profile with the high forehead and flat nose and the dark glasses perched above it that was outlined sharply against the sky. He wondered whether these were the features of their common ancestor, Njangu.

But now he felt they were safe and they would easily get to Mombasa. It would be a great journey for a boy like himself, and when he got home he would have such tales to tell that everyone would listen to him as though he were an elder.

For the first time that day he felt hungry. He'd eaten very little before leaving home because he'd been so worried. Now he untied his bundle and took out a piece of meat wrapped in leaves.

"Will you have some?"

Joshua frowned and grunted. "What are you supposed to be talking about?"

"Oh—I forgot. It's meat. Do you want some?"

Joshua, frowning, shook his head. He seemed to be still on the alert, his nostrils flaring and his mouth moving as though he were constantly muttering to himself.

"The policeman didn't suspect us. We should get to Nairobi safely now."

Still Joshua said nothing, so Mugo began to eat his meat and sweet potato contentedly, gazing out of the window at the strange country they were passing through.

"Jambo!" said the woman in the next seat—the one nursing a baby.

"Msuri."

"Travelling far?"

"A long way."

"You're a good boy to look after that blind man so carefully."

"Well, he's my relative."

The woman nodded. "Families must help each other out."

Mugo also nodded. He was about to ask the woman if she would like to share his meal, when the bus stopped with a suddenness that threw him forward and he felt very indignant as he saw his piece of meat flying through the air in a wild curve and landing on the knees of a passenger some seats ahead.

"Ooi!" he exclaimed, and stood up to get it, and then he saw the dark figure standing in the roadway holding a gun pointed right at the driver. Mugo had seen a man like that before—a man in an animal skin coat with a wild beard and hair falling in little plaits beneath an old felt hat.

There was a fearful murmur among the passengers, and Mugo whispered, "It's a forest fighter!"

"It is Mwengo." Joshua's voice was low and fierce. "It is my enemy. Give me the Decider—quick!"

But it flashed through Mugo's mind that it would be most dangerous to give the gun to Joshua. Without it, they might yet escape from Mwengo, but if Joshua had the gun he would use it, and in a gun fight many people would die.

"I haven't got the Decider," he blurted out.

His uncle turned to glare at him, unbelieving.

"My—my ugly sister buried it—under the maize in her shamba. My father said it was safer."

"Safer? You tick!" muttered Joshua venomously.

His fingers clumsy with fear, Mugo tried to retie his bundle, only too aware of the hard bulk of the Decider in it.

The forest fighter appeared in the doorway. He looked round at the passengers ferociously, his eyes bloodshot. Nobody spoke or moved, but the baby beside Mugo cried and the clink of coins in the conductor's hand was strangely loud. Mugo turned his head nervously to the window and found himself staring into the wild face of another forest fighter. The bus was surrounded.

Mwengo, in the doorway, motioned suddenly with his gun. "Out!" he commanded. "All of you—out!"


"I'm going to make a run for it," murmured Joshua.

Mugo's teeth were chattering as he picked up his bundle but he still protested that if his uncle did that he would ruin everything.

"Act like a blind man—let me lead you. Mwengo mightn't recognize you."

Men with guns—all strangely dressed, wild-looking men —were pushing the frightened passengers into a line along

48

the roadside. The bus had been stopped as it was climbing a steep curve on a heavily wooded stretch of the road—an ideal place for an ambush because there was plenty of cover for the forest fighters and the bus would have to slow down anyway. Behind them the cliff rose steeply, covered in thick undergrowth.

"When the opportunity comes, I shall go up there," muttered Joshua, indicating the cliff.

"What about me?"

There was no reply. Joshua had become as still as a lizard on a stone, his dark glasses gazing ahead, his shoulders stooped over his stick. Mwengo was coming down the line of people, looking closely into face after face. Mugo, as a light breeze shifted the shadows of the leaves that fell about them, caught again the strong smell of the forest fighter.

Suddenly Mwengo gave a signal and two of his men seized one of the passengers and dragged him away, shouting, behind some bushes. There was a low moan from the crowd. They have taken the wrong man, thought Mugo. Or maybe they weren't looking for his uncle after all ... A cascade of shots from the bushes deafened him. A thin, white cloud of smoke puffed up over the leaves and the smell of gunpowder stung his nostrils. Mugo felt sick.

Mwengo smiled with a fierce look of satisfaction.

"He was a traitor. He betrayed two of my men to the police when they came to his village in search of food. All traitors die." And he continued to move down the line peering into each face.

"How long has *he* been blind?"

Mugo glanced fearfully into Mwengo's wide, reddened eyes. His voice, when he spoke, sounded thin and quavering to him—"Many years."

D

Mwengo continued to look closely at Joshua. There was silence except for the baby's crying again, the shuffle of uneasy feet on the road, the soft hissing of the leaves around them.

"Is he dumb as well?"

"No—but a little deaf."

Mwengo continued to stare suspiciously, his eyes dilated, his nostrils moving.

"Tell him to take those glasses off."

"But ... he ... he won't hear ... " stammered Mugo through dry lips.

"*You* take them off then ... "

But Mugo could not move. He could not take those spectacles off and reveal Joshua to Mwengo. Desperately trying to think of an excuse, he grasped his uncle's arm, and suddenly felt it stiffen. At the same time he noticed that Mwengo was standing with raised head as though listening, and after a moment he shouted, "Jeep coming!" and the forest fighters disappeared into the undergrowth as swiftly as a flight of birds into a tree.

"They've gone!" Mugo turned to his uncle, only to find that he had disappeared as well. "Uncle Joshua!" The slight trembling of a bush part way up the cliff gave him a clue, and he followed, pushing his way through the undergrowth. Halfway up the cliff was his uncle, sitting in a bush, his glasses off, panting.

"Get down, boy," he hissed. "Get down and keep still— here is the Jeep."

And round the corner came the Jeep, its tyres screaming to an abrupt halt. And among the policemen in it Mugo saw the long nose and eager eyes of the Homeguard right next to the stern, tanned features of C.I. Mackenzie. Policemen leaped out of the Jeep, and a loud jabbering and crying arose from the crowd.

"Come on," said Mugo's uncle, and began scrambling cautiously upwards.


They paused at the top. Before them stretched a wide field of grain, and further on a meadow with cattle grazing in it, and then a European farmhouse, long and low and glistening white, and to their left a thick, dark woodland that seemed to stretch on and on to the distant blue hills. It was hot, the sun dazzling, and there was only the sound of cattle lowing; but below them was the noisy squabble of voices.

"That was C.I. Mackenzie," panted Mugo, anxiously. "And the Homeguard. In the Jeep. Do your duty diligently *and* scientifically," he added automatically to himself.

"They had their chance and lost it," said his uncle with dry satisfaction and some mystery.

"Their chance of what?"

"Of capturing Mwengo."

"But they were after *you*, not Mwengo."

Joshua did not reply. From below them came the roar of an engine starting up and the grinding of gears.

"That's the bus going on," muttered Joshua.

He was a tall man, Mugo realized, when he stood up straight like that, his head thrown back, his flat nose with the wide nostrils pointing at you, so that it was like looking into the barrels of a shotgun. He was breathing fast and had taken off his glasses. His wounded eye was swollen and half shut with a cut above it, but with his good eye he was gazing swiftly round, every sense trained.

"Where will they be?" asked Mugo anxiously.

His uncle did not seem to hear him.

"That man Mwengo—where will he be?"

His uncle gestured to the trees. "They will keep to that shelter till they reach the thick forest. They won't trouble us again today."

"How can we get to Nakuru to catch the train?"

"We can walk." But he did not sound very interested. He looked at Mugo. "I could get on better without you. You are a liability. You'll draw attention. Look, you go back home now."

Mugo was astonished, and more than that he was deeply hurt. After he had got up the courage to come so far, after his father had carefully drawn up the plan, to have it all suddenly scrapped and himself sent home—how could he face his village and tell them he had not even got as far as Nakuru?

"But you'll need me—especially in Nairobi."

Mugo had a very uncomfortable feeling that his uncle had no intention of keeping to their plan. Suddenly, for some reason, everything had been changed, and he had something else in mind.

"Return home while you can!" And Joshua set off running at a swift rate along a narrow path by the edge of the field. Mugo, hardly able to believe what was happening, watched him going further and further away and saw himself lost. That started him into action, and with a shout to his uncle, he raced after him. But he knew he would never catch him. His uncle, although he was limping badly, ran very fast. And so Mugo began to shout, calling his uncle's name loudly, time after time. And that brought Joshua to a stop. He waited angrily while Mugo, breathless, caught up with him.

"I told you to go home!"

"I'm coming with you," panted Mugo. "I must be with you!"

Joshua seemed to consider this for a few moments, then to Mugo's relief he said, "All right. You lead the way." And he gave Mugo a push along the path.

They went on. It was just a narrow track and rough going under the hot sun. Mugo felt uneasy at the thought of his uncle following behind him. The more he thought about it, the stranger that man seemed. He could move so silently, even with his wounded leg, that Mugo often had the eerie feeling that he wasn't there, and would look back to re-assure himself. And there his uncle would be, limping swiftly and silently along, his dark glasses giving him a truly blind glare.

# 8

MANY times on that walk, Mugo wanted to stop and rest.
The sun beat down on them, and there was very little breeze.
They went almost at a run, for his uncle was constantly
urging him on, and whenever there was the danger of
anyone seeing them, Mugo would find himself suddenly
pulled back into a bush to hide, or walking on alone, his
uncle having disappeared without a word. Mugo was hot
and thirsty and hungry. His feet were sore and his bundle
was heavy, his eyes ached with the glare of the sun, and his
chest ached with the effort of keeping up such a speed. But
his uncle would not rest. He cared nothing for Mugo's
feelings. Mugo began to hate this man who was so ruthless
and who never seemed to tire.

They had left the rich pasture and woodland and were
travelling down through barer country where herds of
zebra passed at a distance, towards the great valley that runs
right through the country from north to south. And suddenly Mugo realized that they were travelling in the wrong
direction. According to the sun they were now travelling
north, but Nakuru, he knew, was in the east.

He stopped.

"Uncle," he said, "we are going the wrong way."

His uncle snorted.

"What do you know about it?"

"But Nakuru is over in that direction."

"Get on, boy … get on!"

Mugo walked on again, but he went thoughtfully, suspicion growing in his mind. He was quite sure they were not travelling towards Nakuru, but why was his uncle lying? Joshua knew the country well—he couldn't be making a mistake. He must be taking the wrong direction quite deliberately. But why? Where was he taking them?

"Get down! Down, you fool!"

Mugo looked round hastily. His uncle had disappeared.

"Get down!"

Then he saw him, crouched under a bush. Bewildered, Mugo ran to another bush and crawled under it. Apart from the slight rustle of the branches, all round was a vast silence underlined by the hiss of the wind through the dry grass. Peering out over the sunlit land, Mugo could see to the east the distant blue shapes of the mountains on the horizon and above them the high, pinkish snows of Kere-Nyaga, the mountain of brightness, where, so Mugo's people believe, lived Ngai. There was no one about, but then Mugo heard a distant humming that turned into a loud, encroaching murmur and beat, like the sound of a swarm of angry hornets. And then he saw, swinging towards them beneath the blue sky, a huge, gleaming insect with wings on its head that spun in a silver circle. Mugo watched in fascinated terror as it swung closer and lower and then hovered above them with a vast beating and murmuring. Mugo had heard of the great planes of the white man, and he had seen them, twice, flying over the village, but he had heard nothing of these giant insects, and he was terrified.

"Joshua—Joshua."

The great insect was speaking in a loud voice above them, shouting his uncle's name.

"Joshua—we know you are there. It is no good hiding from us. You made a promise, Joshua. Keep it!" Then the great insect whirred away and flew off several miles to the north where it stayed again in the blue sky, hovering, as though still watching them.

Mugo did not move for he was held there by his fear of that great insect. And his uncle also did not seem to exist any more, he had merged so successfully with the bush he was under. Then, after what seemed a long time, Mugo saw that bush shake and his uncle crawled out. He stood up, dusting leaves and soil from his coat, and then straightened up and gazed with a steady glare of hatred towards the great insect, seemingly not at all afraid that it might see him. Then, in an almost sulky way, and without a word to Mugo, he swung round and went at a lope towards the east.

When Mugo saw that, his limbs were unfrozen, he scrambled out of the bush and raced after his uncle. Joshua did not stop, and indeed it was some time before Mugo caught up with him, his black face shiny with sweat, his shirt clinging wetly to his back. By then the great insect had disappeared from the sky, and the houses of Nakuru had appeared among the clusters of trees by the side of the flamingo lake.

"What was it, Uncle?" Mugo demanded breathlessly. "The voice from the great insect—what was it? What does it mean?"

"It's no business of yours," retorted Joshua, putting on the dark glasses which he hadn't bothered with since the insect shouted at them.

"But what was it? I've never seen anything like it … And it knew you! How did it … "

"That was a helicopter. It belongs to the white men. Now stop asking so many questions, you small rat. You are only fit for herding goats."

"That's not true," retorted Mugo. "I am almost a **man**."

"Do not argue."

Mugo was silent. It was wrong, he knew, to argue with his elders, but his uncle's refusal to answer his questions only made him more suspicious. It was not his uncle who was blind, it was himself, because he no longer knew what was going on. Who was it shouting from the helicopter? And what was in his uncle's mind when he took the direction away from Nakuru? Suspicions gnawed more strongly than hunger at his stomach. But then his uncle said, "You must lead me again. This is Nakuru. We will have to go more slowly," and Mugo felt relieved. They would catch the train at Nakuru as his father had planned. All would be well.

They went on towards the town, and Mugo began to hope that in the train he would be able to eat some of the food in his bundle and perhaps get some water to drink. But before they reached Nakuru he heard a distant rumbling sound and saw the long silver line of the snake that spits fire sliding across the floor of the valley towards the town.

"The train—Uncle! There is the train!"

"Yes," said his uncle sourly, "there is the train." But he made no attempt to quicken his pace.

It was Mugo who, running ahead of his uncle, reached the station with its deep, shadowy interior, just as the rumbling and snorting started again and the train for Nairobi slid from the platform. A guard with his flag and whistle was turning away with the air of a man who has done a good job, and good or not, it was the only job he did each day, there being only one train a day to Nairobi. Mugo ran forward shouting, "Stop it! Stop the train!"

"Stop the train!" exclaimed the guard in disgust. "You've come in from the bush, boy, if you don't know we can't stop the Nairobi train."

"But I have to get to Nairobi—"

"Then you'll have to wait for the next train—and that will be tomorrow."

He walked away with slow dignity.

The train disappeared from sight, and gradually the roar of its passage dwindled into a thin mutter across the great valley. The little shadowy station with the sun gleaming on the silver rails was quite silent, growing hotter and sleepier as the heat of the afternoon drew on. Mugo stood by the side of the track, his ears dulled by the growing silence, feeling oppressed by the emptiness of the station, and with his gaze fixed on the figure of his uncle who stood leaning on his stick in the arched entrance to the station. Against the bright sunshine outside he looked like a black sentinel, his head thrown back.

Mugo was filled with a sudden rage against him.

"It's *your* fault!" he shouted, and his voice echoed and grew to giant size in the hollow building. "It's all your fault!" He rushed across to Joshua, dancing in his anger and frustration and weariness before that still, blind figure. "You wouldn't walk fast enough! You wouldn't hurry! And you deliberately took the wrong direction. You didn't mean to catch the train, did you? You never meant to catch it. You don't mean to go to Nairobi or Mombasa. You have something else in mind!"

"Now then, now then, boy," tutted the station-master looking out of the door of his office at them. "I won't have this kind of noise in my station. You should be ashamed to speak to a blind man in that way. Where were you brought up?"

"Blind!" exclaimed Mugo in exasperation. "Blind! He sees more than we do. I tell you … " He stopped himself and slumped against the wall, exhausted and tired and hungry. "Well," he said, more calmly and more determined, "we are going to Mombasa. Whatever you think. And now we'll just have to *walk* to Nairobi."

For all the notice Joshua had taken of this Mugo might just as well not have spoken. "Come," he said, and grasped Mugo's arm firmly, and they began to walk slowly down the road from the station into the town.

Mugo had never been in a town before, and he had always wanted to see the paved streets and glass-windowed shops, the hotel and churches of Nakuru. But now he was too exhausted to notice them. As his uncle directed, he led the way to the far end of the town where a street of buildings with corrugated iron roofs straggled along the railway line. They stopped opposite the Good Friends Bar which was next to the Indian tailor's where customers and sewing-machines shared the verandah. For a few moments they paused under the shade of a tree while Joshua examined the open-fronted bar, busy with men pushing in and out, eating, drinking and talking, lounging in the sun outside. A plump and perspiring girl in a red cotton dress and headscarf went from the tables to the kitchen carrying trays piled with plates and glasses.

59

Mugo, completely exhausted, had sunk on to a bench under the tree, his mind for the moment dulled by weariness and hunger.

"Big Black John owns that bar."

Mugo looked up at his uncle. Joshua, gazing ahead, seemed to be speaking to himself in a low, monotonous voice.

"He was my friend, once. A friend to all of us. But will he still be my friend? That's the question."

"We could have some food—rest for a while."

"I'll have to risk it. He's essential to my plan."

Mugo stared dully at the bar opposite. Will Big Black John help us to get to Nairobi, he wondered.

"It looks safe," murmured Joshua. "I see no faces I recognize—none of Mwengo's followers. And yet I feel danger." He scanned the shop for a few more minutes, then he put out his hand to Mugo. "Lead me across."

They crossed the road slowly, approaching the bar, Mugo leading his uncle, who was limping and leaned heavily on his stick.

"Find a table and help me to sit down."

Mugo was trembling. The thought of the police frightened him, but so also did the thought of Mwengo and the forest fighters, and they could be disguised as ordinary people. He led his uncle into the hot and crowded bar and helped him to sit at a table. After a while, the girl in the red dress came to take their order and Joshua ordered two cups of tea and asked if he could speak to Big Black John. The girl, casting a sympathetic look at the blind man and the boy, went into the kitchen, and a few moments later a huge, very dark man appeared in the doorway, looking over the customers.

"Is that Big Black John?" asked Mugo.

"Shut up!" hissed his uncle. "Don't draw any more attention to us."

Mugo was offended. "I wasn't going to," he retorted. "If anybody draws attention to us, it will be you. You look as if you're going to be sick."

"It's the smell of people. I can't stand the smell of people in crowds after living so long in the forests."

Mugo greedily drank the tea the girl brought. It was such a relief to be sitting there out of the sun. Now if he could only have some food ...

"You smelt pretty horrible yourself," he said, "before you had a wash."

"The smell of soap and tobacco—I can't stand it." Joshua sat back in his chair. "Here's Big Black John. Be quiet."

Mugo watched Big Black John moving among the customers, chatting to this one and that one, casting sharp glances at Mugo and his uncle and then, very casually, stopping at their table.

"Jambo," he said. "Travelling far?"

"We travel far, but slowly. What more would you expect of a blind man and a boy?"

"Dangerous times to be travelling anyway."

Mugo's uncle did not reply. Staring straight ahead, and not in Big John's direction, he said in a quiet voice, "I have a message from a friend of yours who would like your help."

"I am always willing to help a friend." Big Black John looked closely at Joshua and then at Mugo. Mugo met his gaze, trying not to look as though he was afraid.

"Please join us," said Joshua.

# 9

BIG BLACK JOHN eased himself on to the small chair. "Well?"

"Do you remember Joshua?"

Big Black John nodded, staring out through the front of the shop to the sun-drenched, dusty street. "Joshua, I have heard, is in great trouble," he said. "He has made an enemy of Mwengo."

"He did not mean to," protested Mugo's uncle.

"Mwengo is mad. He believes Joshua tried to kill him."

"It was an accident. Joshua's gun went off by accident and the bullet just missed Mwengo."

"Still, Mwengo is mad. He says, so I am told, that he will hunt Joshua down."

The two men sat thoughtfully, saying nothing. Mugo looked from face to face anxiously. At last his uncle said, "Mwengo *is* mad. There are so few fighters left in the forest now. They have nearly all been captured or killed. Mwengo has only about twenty followers, yet he still believes he is chosen by God, by Ngai, to be the leader of our country."

Big Black John shrugged his shoulders. "What is it Joshua wants?" he asked.

"Can you get a message from him into the forest—to Mwengo?"

Mugo looked at his uncle in astonishment. A message to Mwengo? To his enemy?

Big Black John shook his head. "I cannot. As you said, there are fewer men in the forest now, and the police watch everyone here very carefully to stop us helping them. I have no means of getting anything through to Mwengo."

Joshua did not seem troubled. "Ah well," he said, "it is not so important. But perhaps you can help in another way. Can you get Joshua to Naivasha?"

"Not Naivasha," Mugo interrupted. "Nairobi."

His uncle turned on him, snarling, "Hyena! Will you be silent?"

Mugo was indignant. "But we're going to … "

"Hyena!"

Mugo was silent, beginning to think his uncle, like Mwengo, was mad.

Big Black John listened to this with interest, and now said soothingly, "It will not be easy, my friend, to get Joshua to Nairobi or Naivasha. There is a lot of police activity at present. But if you can wait here for a while, I'll make some inquiries."

Big Black John stood up, heaving his body out of the chair, his broad, smiling face gazing round warily at his customers.

"Big Black John." Mugo's uncle spoke very quietly, but his voice made Big Black John pause. "*I* am Joshua."

Big Black John slowly sat down again, looking hard at Joshua. Then he sat back and looked again out at the street.

"You know, man," he said, "I didn't recognize you."

"We are not going to Naivasha," said Mugo firmly to his uncle. "We are going to Nairobi."

"I know what I'm doing. Naivasha is on the way to Nairobi. You are ignorant, boy."

But in spite of the insult, Mugo was satisfied. They were continuing the journey. It was all that mattered.

Big Black John had left them to make arrangements. They sat without speaking. But suddenly Mugo was aware that his uncle was sitting very still and tense. He waited, schooling himself to keep silent, watching his uncle's face anxiously.

"I have a feeling. There's something wrong here."

Mugo looked round the café. "Everything seems all right," he said.

"I still have a feeling ... "

Big Black John was away for about ten minutes. Then he sat down with them again and gave Joshua a significant nod.

"I think I can arrange something," he said. "There will be a taxi waiting for you in an hour's time at the end of the town. It will take you to Naivasha. Until then, you can stay here."

"I'm grateful, Big Black John."

The two men sat talking in low voices, their heads close together, about the battle of the forest fighters and the terrible things that had happened. "Put into detention—it was a homeguard picked him up ... He was shot in the back, we had to leave him by a stream ... he must have died ... Mwengo strangled him ... he was pushed into an ant-bear hole ... "

Fascinated by these horrifying details, Mugo's dark eyes steadily watched the faces of the two men, his own face expressionless, until the bar filled with the smell of a very savoury stew, and these details became less important than his stomach protesting that it was empty.

"Uncle," he interrupted at last. "I have not eaten since early this morning."

"You have food in your bundle."

Mugo stooped to untie his bundle that lay at his feet, but there was no food in it—not even a sweet potato.

"The food has gone! I've lost it. It must have fallen on the floor of the bus when it stopped ... " Mugo could have cried with disappointment. He was so very hungry.

Big Black John smiled. "You shall eat here—at my charge. You must not go hungry," and he called the girl over and ordered a plate of stew for each of them.

After that, Mugo felt, for the moment, quite content, considering how pleasant it was not to be hungry any longer, to be sitting in comfort instead of tramping after his uncle for mile after mile, to have the prospect of riding in a taxi to Naivasha. Idly he watched the hens scratching in the dust of the street, a man being shaved by a wayside barber, a woman and her daughter seated on the ground and selling the vegetables spread out before them, the poster with the photograph on it pasted on the lamp-post outside the shop ...

Mugo sat up, suddenly wide awake, staring at the poster. He could just make out that the photograph was of his uncle Joshua in the beard he had worn in the forest and with his hair in plaits. And the only words he could read were those over the picture—"£600 Reward".

Mugo looked quickly at his uncle. He did not seem to have noticed it, but Big Black John—surely *his* eyes were fixed in a dreamy stare on that photograph? If he knew about it, if he knew Joshua was wanted and a big reward was offered—why hadn't he said so? Mugo was suddenly suspicious of the big, kindly man. He looked into Big Black John's face more carefully. Weren't his eyes full of cunning above the smile? Was he planning to betray them?

"Uncle—we should go," he said urgently.

"There is still some time … "

"I think we should not sit too long in one place …"

Mugo was quite certain now. Big Black John was after that reward.

Big Black John nodded his head.

"The boy is right, Joshua. People soon notice things, and the police are always watchful."

Mugo heard his uncle sigh, and for the first time he noticed that his face looked weary and that there was a line between his brows that could have been a line of pain.

"Very well." He stood up slowly. "We'll go on. Thank you, Big Black John. I will not", he added significantly, "forget you."

For a few moments Big Black John looked up at him as though he were not quite sure of Joshua's meaning. Then he smiled again, shook hands and watched them go along the street of the shanty town.

## 10

THEY crouched under the shade of a tree together, squatting on their haunches, their eyes turned towards the road from Nakuru along which the taxi would come. Mugo felt hot and sleepy after his meal, and Joshua smoked a cigarette. And as he sat there by the empty road with the vastness of the big valley beyond him, Mugo scanned his uncle's features again, thinking of whether Joshua looked like Njangu, wondering where he had gone, that fervent, smooth-faced young man who had spoken of freedom so rousingly that day. The thin, twisted face with the dark glasses concealing the eyes seemed to bear no relation to that earlier face.

And because he still feared Joshua, and because Joshua had told him he must learn to hold his tongue, he wondered whether he should mention his suspicions about Big Black John. Would Joshua simply think him stupid? But surely he must say something?

"Can you trust Big Black John?" he asked tentatively.

Joshua looked grimly away. "I can trust nobody."

"You *can't* trust him." There was no reply. Joshua shifted uneasily again as though he were in pain. "They're offering a reward for you—they've pasted your picture up ..."

His uncle muttered to himself. Mugo could not make out

clearly what he was saying. It seemed to be about Mwengo. Did Mwengo, Mugo wondered, have the evil in his blood? Was he really mad? Or did they just say that? A sudden urgency took hold of him, a conviction that his uncle must be warned.

"Big Black John knows about the reward—the poster was just outside his bar—he was looking at it. Don't you see, he must mean to betray us for the reward ... "

"I know all this. Do you think I've no eyes and no instincts? I know Big Black John."

"Then what are we sitting here for? Waiting for the police? Or Mwengo?"

Joshua threw away the stub of his cigarette. He sat more comfortably, leaning back against the tree, his legs stretched out before him.

"Big Black John will betray us—not to Mwengo, there'd be no money in that. He'll betray us to the police. Still, we'll take this taxi. It will come, because Big Black John wouldn't want us to be arrested right on his doorstep. That would give him away. The hyena doesn't follow the lion too closely."

And Big Black John had seemed such a friend. Mugo pondered on his duplicity.

"The taxi, I should think, will take us almost to Naivasha," said Joshua thoughtfully. "Then the police will arrive. And that is nothing to worry about." He muttered again to himself, gazing straight ahead, his lips hardly moving. At last he said quietly, "The police will learn that I wanted to send a message to Mwengo—and that I am going to Naivasha. That is satisfactory."

Mugo could not see what was satisfactory about it. The wide, flat bottom of the valley with its chain of lakes and extinct volcanoes, shimmered before his eyes in the heat of the afternoon, and the cloud shadows sped silently over it. Already, he thought, they had been travelling since sunrise, and if things had gone as they planned they would have been in Nairobi instead of sitting under that tree by the roadside waiting for treachery to strike. What was his uncle planning? How were they to avoid the police? Instinctively, remembering the Decider, he stretched out his hand to his bundle, wondering whether he shouldn't hide it there by the roadside instead of risking being caught with it.

"I wish you'd never gone into the forest!" he blurted out, suddenly overcome by all the difficulties of their situation and tracing them all back to Joshua.

"There was freedom to be won for my country. But you're too young to understand that." Joshua could spit out contempt quite suddenly.

"But before that even," insisted Mugo, "you left our village — the home of our people."

"Home? If I have a home it is in the forests over yonder on the far side of the valley. Yes, if I have a home it is there."

His voice was so unusually gentle that Mugo looked at him as he crouched against a tree, alert and hunted.

"But you can't go back there," Mugo insisted.

"There is happiness in the green light of the forest. Security in the great thickets of bamboo, and there is community among the animals. They were our friends. Ngai was with us in the forest." Joshua's shoulders suddenly straightened, and his voice became harsh. "And I was a leader there, equal to Mwengo. I *could* have been equal to him. Mwengo is mad. He thought he was God's chosen! Eeei!" He spat contemptuously. "God's chosen! Because of Mwengo I'm a hunted creature ... The taxi is coming." His words dropped harshly into the complete silence of the great valley.

The taxi was not new and it approached them noisily. Remembering what his uncle had said about not trusting anyone, Mugo looked hard at the driver, but he seemed an ordinary enough African. But he had also looked carefully at them.

"Big Black John is paying," he said, "and I will take you to Naivasha. But there is a lot of police activity on the road. If we are stopped—remember, I just picked you up on the road. I know nothing about you," and he drove off at an alarming rate, sending up a cloud of red dust.

Where the road was poor, Mugo and Joshua hung on desperately, and where it was good, they also hung on desperately as the car shied round corners and hovered over the edges of cliffs. They plunged down the valley towards Naivasha.

Suddenly, Mugo heard his uncle shouting. "Stop here— here. I'm telling you, man—stop!"

"But Big Black John said … "

"Never mind Big Black John … "

The taxi stopped, and Mugo saw the reason why. Joshua had produced a *simi*—a two-edged knife—and was holding it in the ribs of the quaking driver. Mugo sat completely still, waiting for the *simi* to be plunged in and for Joshua to taste the blood of his enemy.

"I've done nothing, man," the driver protested.

"You will tell me. Big Black John told you who I was, didn't he?"

"Well, yes … "

"And he offered to split the reward, didn't he?"

The man nodded, sweat gleaming on his brow.

"I expected it. What was the plan? He has told the police? Were they to stop us—outside Naivasha?"

"Yes—they said a police check, or maybe a Jeep would stop us, they said ... but it was Big Black John's idea ... "

"I will remember you, man," said Joshua. "And I will remember Big Black John. Tell him that. Come on, boy."

They scrambled out of the car, but as they did so a Jeep appeared from the direction of Nakuru, travelling swiftly towards them. As it got nearer, Mugo easily recognized in it the stern, tanned features of the European and the long nose of the man next to him. "It is C.I. Mackenzie! And the Homeguard!"

There was no time to escape. The Jeep was almost upon them. They watched as it approached, but strangely it did not slow down. It swept on towards them and Mugo stared straight into the face of the Homeguard who was standing up, waving his rifle at them and shouting and gesturing, with C.I. Mackenzie hanging on to him as though trying to stop him jumping out. As they passed, the Homeguard levelled his gun at Joshua, but C.I. Mackenzie knocked it upwards so that the gun fired into the air, and the Jeep swept on round the corner. The sound of the gunshot reverberated throughout the valley and a herd of impala deer behind them started into swift life and a host of sunset-coloured flamingoes rose, shrieking, like small clouds over the trees round the distant lake, and subsided again.

"Come on," said Joshua, and Mugo needed no second telling. Together they loped away over the grass and through the bushes, north-eastwards, skirting Naivasha and with the high, forested slopes of the mountains before them, two small, dark figures lost in a vast, yellow-green stretch of plain.

It was late afternoon. They sat down together by a stream under the shelter of some trees. Around them the hot air was loud with insects, the wide, dry valley shimmered in heat. South of them ran the narrow silver line of the railway towards Naivasha, with its lake beyond, and on to Nairobi.

Mugo's leg muscles ached from the long walk, his feet were cut and bleeding and swollen—he hardly recognized them as his feet, as they stretched out beyond his trouser legs. His mouth was parched and his stomach empty, and he was sticky with sweat. He laid his head back against the tree trunk and closed his eyes. His mind was bewildered by weariness and doubt. Soon it would be nightfall—they had travelled all day. They should soon have been getting on the train that ran each night from Nairobi to Mombasa. Instead, they were lost here, not even at Naivasha. They had travelled about thirty-five miles, and still had over fifty to go before Nairobi. And they couldn't possibly go by rail or road.

"I'm hungry—and thirsty," he murmured in protest.

Joshua rolled his face towards him. He seemed about to speak, then he rolled his face away again.

How would they avoid the police? Avoid them? Mugo shook his head, trying to wake his brain up again. Didn't it seem as though it was the police avoiding them? Hadn't the C.I. driven past them, and stopped the Homeguard shooting Joshua? It must all be a dream—a nightmare. Mugo looked cautiously at the silent figure leaning back against the tree, legs stretched out, completely still. Was Joshua concerned? He said it was satisfactory that Big Black John had told the police about them. How could it be satisfactory? And who had shouted at him from the helicopter? And where—where had Joshua been trying to go to?

Joshua moaned, took off his glasses with a weary gesture and rubbed his hand over his face. He looked down at his wounded leg. There was a dark stain on the trouser leg, and flies buzzed round it and crawled over it. Joshua began struggling to his feet. When he put his weight on his leg, he stumbled, groaning again, and leaning back against the tree. He saw Mugo's wide, mystified eyes on him.

"Better do something about this. Bathe it. Stream over there."

"I'll help you ... " Mugo scrambled up, forcing his stiff legs to obey him, but Joshua pushed him away.

"I don't need help." He began limping away towards the stream, crooked and bent, his long coat flapping behind him.

Mugo went after him.

"Wait—I've got a new shirt in my bundle—my sister packed it for me to wear in Nairobi. It'll make a good bandage ... "

Joshua paused, not looking back.

"And we could wash your trousers—there'll be enough sun still to dry them ... "

"You have some sense," said his uncle.

As he searched in his bundle for the shirt, Mugo's hands encountered the hard steel of the Decider. For a moment he thought of giving it back to Joshua. They were in such danger, perhaps Joshua should have the gun. But he thought again of Njangu and wondered how far he could trust Joshua, and pushed the gun away.


They sat once more under the tree. Joshua's face was drawn with pain, and Mugo, still feeling sick as he had done at the sight of his uncle's wound, wondered how he had walked so far; from knee to ankle his leg was swollen, with blood seeping from the bullet wound, and the skin tight and shiny. It must, Mugo thought, have been excruciatingly painful and Joshua had panted and moaned as he bathed and bandaged it. Mugo had washed his trousers and they now hung in the branches of the tree to dry.

"Perhaps we should go back home," he suggested.

"We go on."

"You can't walk on that leg—we must get some help."

"Go on … " muttered Joshua.

The sun was moving towards the west. Darkness would be falling, and they were stranded in the vastness of the valley, without food and a prey to wild animals.

"The thing to do is", said Mugo, trying to keep his voice steady and matter-of-fact, "find a way of getting to Nairobi quickly."

"We must go into the forest."

Joshua's voice was quite calm, but Mugo was shocked.

"The forest?"

"It's the only way. I know the forest well. We can travel through it, over the shoulder of the mountain and down to Nairobi. The journey will be longer, but there is no other way." He cast a sidelong glance at Mugo as though he were curious to see his reaction.

Mugo had only one thought. "It's too dangerous. There's Mwengo … "

Joshua did not seem to think Mwengo mattered. "The forest is big enough," he said.

"There must be another way … "

"If—if it wasn't for this leg, I wouldn't need you!" Joshua exclaimed. "For a time you'll stay," he ordered.

74

To the east, the flat bottom of the great valley stretched for twenty miles to the escarpment, the steep cliff above which hung the forests that clothed the mountain sides.

It's too far and too dangerous, thought Mugo. Perhaps my uncle is mad, like Mwengo. Anyway, he can't walk so far on his wounded leg.

"We will rest tonight," said Joshua, as though reading his thoughts, "and start early tomorrow. I'll have to travel slowly."

Mugo was filled with fear and desperation at the way the journey was changing in the hands of this man who had the evil in his blood. He felt completely helpless and cheated. "I think," he blurted out, "I think it's a trick. You never meant to go to Mombasa. You didn't mean to follow the plan."

Joshua did not reply immediately. Then he said slowly, "I will not deny that it might be a trick. All of it. I have made certain promises which must be kept. And I suppose I could manage without you. But this wound is worse now, and I may need help. Your father would not approve of you deserting me."

Mugo knew he would have to go on—he had no other choice, but he began to be determined to watch this tricky man very carefully, as carefully as Joshua was now observing the distant countryside.

"We can drink from the stream there. And there are huts over in that direction with shambas nearby. After dark we can dig up some vegetables. We won't starve."

## I I

THEY travelled across the floor of the valley towards the vast wall of the escarpment over which hung heavy, dark woods. Above the woods lay the summits, hidden in clouds. They walked on all next day through the hot sunlight, over the coarse red soil, and tufty, brittle grasses. Sad-eyed giraffes looked down at them over umbrella thorns, and blue and orange lizards scuttled away from them to the safety of stones, and herds of zebra cantered past. Sometimes they would come upon a herd of cattle, and then Mugo's uncle would warn him to go cautiously, to avoid herdsmen and the possibility of a village. Occasionally, Mugo would look back towards the west, shading his eyes from the sun that still flooded the flat length of the great valley, in the direction of the lake and his village, wistfully thinking of his father and sisters, and then he would turn to look with a sense of the unbelievable towards those great mountains he was supposed to cross.

Once they encountered the branch line of the railway, a narrow, single track, winding through the dry scrub grass, and several times they passed women bent double by huge bundles supported by straps round their foreheads on their way to a village deep in the interior. Apart from this, they saw no one. No sign of the police or of Mwengo, so that Mugo felt more and more that he was living some kind of nightmare in which they were running away from nothing but an unexplained fear, and were running to an unknown place. He seemed bound by invisible chains to that tall, dark figure that limped heavily forward, relentlessly, never ceasing, in front of him.

They carried with them a few of the potatoes they had stolen, and when he was very hungry Mugo nibbled at one, but eventually he could take no more; the very smell of them made him feel sick, and he preferred to go hungry.

The sky began to cloud, bringing no immediate relief from the heat, but only an increasing breathlessness. It looked as though it would rain eventually, but just then Mugo and Joshua were hot, tired and thirsty, and Mugo was growing more and more fearful as the steep wall of the escarpment drew nearer.

At last Mugo could go no further. He dropped down beside an outcrop of rocks, and sat with his head drooping between his knees. His head throbbed, bright sparks danced before his eyes, his throat was parched and his whole body ached. Joshua, turning, saw that he had stopped and limped back.

"There isn't much further to go today," he said. "We'll stay in one of the huts in a village just over the next ridge."

Mugo raised his eyes to judge the distance. It seemed a long way over the plain that shimmered in the warm breeze.

"One of the villagers used to help the forest fighters. I've stayed there before."

Mugo licked his lips with a dry tongue. "But," he said in a voice that was more like a croak, "but—isn't it dangerous? He might send a message to Mwengo that you're there."

"He might."

"But ... " Mugo could not understand this, "if Mwengo

knows—he'll be waiting for you when you go into the forest."

Joshua ignored him. "We cannot approach the hut until after dark. We mustn't be seen. We'll wait here till sunset."

There was no moon that night, and though gradually Mugo's eyes became accustomed to the darkness, the valley was still to him a stretch of variegated shade until a darker hump loomed before them. The dark shape proved to be a thickly woven thorn hedge round a sleeping village. Joshua led the way into the village, moving silently among the huts. Mugo could not understand how he moved so silently and found his way so easily in the dark.

There was a scratching noise as his uncle moved his fingers over the wooden window of one hut. After a moment or two a voice inside called quietly, "It is late. Go away." Mugo's heart sank. They were not going to find shelter. But his uncle didn't seem disturbed. After a pause he scratched again, and then they heard bolts being slid back and the slight creak as a door opened. Joshua moved like a shadow through the opening, and Mugo followed quickly and more clumsily.

The room was smoky and shadowy, lit only from the fire on the hearth of stones where a pot of food cooked. Opposite the door a blanket hung from two bamboo poles. The man who had let them in bolted the door again and went to sit by the fire, looking up at them, his face shadowed and twisted by the flames.

Joshua squatted at the other side of the fire, and motioned Mugo to do the same. For a while nothing was said. Mugo nodded sleepily in the warmth. The hiss of green wood burning was in his ears, and the strong smoke filled his nostrils and stung his eyes.

Then the man spoke. He had a narrow face, like a rat's, and he looked up at Joshua out of small, bright eyes. "You are not from the forest?"

"You are expecting someone from the forest," replied Joshua.

The man chuckled. "Then you *are* from the forest. You knew the password and the way of scratching twice, and you know what I am waiting for, with food ready."

"I know you," said Joshua, broodingly. "You are Kiongo. You supply food to Mwengo's army."

The man frowned suspiciously at that. "Who *are* you?" he asked. "What has brought you here?"

"We need help and a shelter for the night." Joshua rolled up the leg of his trousers and began to unwind the bandage on his wounded leg. A terrible smell came from the wound, and when it was uncovered, Mugo saw that the leg was one long suppurating sore where the swelling had burst. Mugo felt dizzy and sick at the sight and the appalling stench in the small, hot hut.

How had he walked on it? he thought in dismay. What kind of man was Joshua? Was he human at all?

Kiongo seemed undisturbed. "You have been wounded, that's clear. I shouldn't be surprised if a wound like that killed you."

"Get me water to bathe it ... "

Kiongo shuffled about, fetching a gourd from a corner. "I can do better than that." He scattered herbs into hot water and bathed Joshua's leg very gently, but Joshua had to grit his teeth to bear it. Then he wrapped leaves round the wound and bound it with another strip of Mugo's shirt.

"I seem to remember you," said Kiongo, watching Joshua, "but I haven't seen you for some time."

"Give us some food," panted Joshua, "and let the boy here sleep. We've travelled all day, and last night we slept under bushes in the open. Later, I'll tell you who I am."

Kiongo grinned and nodded. He gave them food and then showed Mugo a mattress lying behind the blanket. Mugo tumbled on to it, and fell into a deep sleep.

He wakened suddenly, aware that something had disturbed him, and he heard Kiongo's voice: "It is late. Go away." Then came the scratch on the shutter again and Mugo heard the door beyond the blanket open.

There followed the mutter of voices, and some exclamations and scuffling. Mugo leapt to the end of the mattress. There was a slit in the blanket and he peered through cautiously. In the shadowy space round the fire he could see his uncle standing threateningly, the *simi* in his hand, and beside the door stood two forest fighters, their guns lying at their feet, watching Joshua warily. Kiongo squatted by the three hearthstones, shaking his head, stirring the food in the pot.

"It is nothing, nothing," he was saying. "He means no danger to you. He wants only to give you a message."

"It is Joshua," said one of the fighters. "Rhino! What do you want? When Mwengo finds you he will strangle you and leave your body for the hyenas!"

"Mwengo will not find me until I choose." Joshua's voice was low and firm. "Sit down. I'll talk to you."

"And you, you rat," a forest fighter spat at Kiongo, "Mwengo will be told you have betrayed us—you will be cut into pieces!"

Kiongo shrugged. "Only listen to him … "

80

The men squatted by the fire and Joshua began to talk. His voice was quiet but persuasive.

"I was not trying to kill Mwengo—I would never wish to kill him ... "

"The shot scorched his jacket ... "

"I was cleaning my gun, my Decider—it was an accident ... Listen to me, I'm only asking you to take a message to Mwengo ... "

Mugo held his breath, listening more carefully.

"You know what Mwengo will do if we take a message from you? He will strangle us like goats—just for speaking to you he would strangle us like goats!"

"And stuff our bodies down ant-bear holes!"

"He would beat us with stinging nettles until our bodies were swollen and sore ... "

The voices, which had risen in protest, dropped to a murmur again, and Mugo missed what was said, but it seemed that the men at last agreed, for Joshua seemed to relax. And in the quiet Mugo heard his voice clearly.

"I want to come back to the forest. Tell Mwengo that. Only tell him that! Take him this message from Joshua— Joshua is loyal, he wishes to come back."

Mugo could not believe it. Joshua had said he would kill Mwengo. He had told his father that.

"Mwengo is my friend, my general." Mugo had never heard Joshua's voice so smooth and persuasive. "Tell him that."

The men stirred and grumbled uneasily.

"Listen then," he went on. "I must know what Mwengo thinks of this, so you must leave a message for me. I will not come near Mwengo till I have his word that he has forgiven me. If he has, leave a message in the valley where

F

two waterfalls are heard at the same time, just below where the black forest meets the bamboo. There is an elephant's skull lying among the undergrowth. Tell Mwengo to leave a message in the skull, and I will find it."

There was some further murmuring, and the men prepared to leave. "Do not think Mwengo will agree," they said. "Mwengo does not forget or forgive an enemy."

They picked up their skin bags which Kiongo had filled with food, and the big pieces of roast meat that he had wrapped carefully in leaves. The door was opened again and they disappeared into the night.

Mugo sank back on the bed. What was he to believe? That Joshua meant to return to Mwengo? Yet he had told the village elders that he wanted to escape. And C.I. Mackenzie drove past and did not try to capture Joshua. His uncle was cunning as a monkey. There was a great deal he, Mugo, didn't know, but he began to understand why Joshua hadn't wanted him with him. But now they were to go into the forest the next day with Mwengo expecting them, waiting for them. They would almost certainly be killed. And if they weren't—if Mwengo took Joshua back— what would happen then to Mugo? He began to realize that he was in a trap, and there seemed no way out. He thought of escaping in the early morning as soon as Joshua and Kiongo slept. But then the memory of the long miles they had travelled over the empty land came to him. Suppose Joshua chased him and killed him so that he could not go back and tell his father?

And he might be wrong—Joshua's plans might be deeper and more complicated and he might not intend any harm to Mugo after all.

Thinking it all over, Mugo decided stubbornly to stick it

out a little longer. He would not run back home too soon. And besides, he still had the Decider. He would go on with Joshua, then, but he would learn to be as wary as his uncle. He would watch him. Cautiously, he got up again to peer through the blanket.

Joshua and Kiongo remained squatting by the fire, the flames throwing flickering lights over their thoughtful faces, the smoke wreathing shadowily about their heads. Mugo shivered as he watched, with the morning chill and the fear of his uncle.

"You cannot trust Mwengo," said Kiongo at last. "He has the cunning of a monkey, and he does not forgive."

"I do not expect him to."

Kiongo shrugged again.

Mugo did not sleep again that night. When the light of dawn began to filter through into the hut, his uncle called to him that they must go before the village wakened, and Mugo got up and fastened up his bundle, ate some breakfast and followed Joshua into the cold half-light. The village was like a ghost village about them.

They had not travelled far over the dark plain when the sky began to streak with rose over the mountains before them and the sun came up, a dull, red ball. The plain was like a great sea and the wind rippled the grasses like waves. Through the crystalline air came, from a distant clump of trees, a loud jabbering, and as they reached the trees, a cloud of thornbills detached themselves like pieces of charred paper from a bonfire flung into the sky by a passing wind.

They spoke very little as they followed the narrow track

that led towards the escarpment. Joshua went ahead, no longer the blind man, but limping heavily, and Mugo followed, his bundle bumping against his shoulder, his uncle's coat always ahead of him flapping in the breeze, and the space between them and the mountains and the forest lessened. And, as though for their amusement, once, as they rested, a crowd of cranes in their grey feathers and black skull-caps danced a strange ballet before them, bouncing lightly on their long legs, as though they were held by elastic to the earth, and then suddenly breaking away into the sky.

Once Mugo heard the strange beating sound, and looking up into the brilliance of the sky he saw the helicopter hanging there to the north of them. His uncle paid it no attention. He did not run to hide, but went on, with a kind of defiance, still limping, his coat still flapping. And Mugo said nothing. He had no energy for talking, and he was too troubled in his mind for argument. But he noticed when the helicopter, as though satisfied, swung away down the sky towards the west.

It seemed quite suddenly that they were standing at the foot of the great cliff that marked the eastern end of the valley, and there they paused.

"We are almost safe," said Joshua.

Mugo looked up at what seemed a sheer face of rock.

"How can we get up there?" he asked.

"It's not difficult."

But it was. Sometimes they crept along narrow tracks that cut steeply up the escarpment side; sometimes they climbed over rocks and boulders that were rough and hot on their bare skin; sometimes Mugo would cling, panting, to a straggly bush and look back fearfully at the steep and rocky cliff that fell away beneath them. And then he would be dizzy and sick, and wish he had never started on this nightmare journey with his uncle. But at last they clambered, exhausted, over the edge where the woods hung heavily on the higher slopes and the air was cooler.

After hours of climbing, they stood at last, breathless, on the cliff looking down to where the purple shadows of clouds still marched over the valley floor, over the distant gleam of the lake and the round humps of extinct volcanoes. The whole valley seemed in motion with the clouds that rolled slowly across the high, blue sky. From where they stood, it was difficult to believe that men and animals existed on that vast, deep plain.

Behind and around them rose the forest-clad slopes, gouged by deep rifts, cut by clear streams, haunted by numerous animals—and by the forest fighters.

They dropped on to the grass, too tired to speak. Mugo saw a flash of azure and green and purple across a flat stone as an iguana slid away from them. And Mugo remembered an iguana his father had once killed and how the brilliant colours had drained away as the creature died and left nothing but a grey, lifeless lump. It seemed to him that his uncle was in some ways a mystery like the iguana, one moment a flashing mystery of conflicting ideas and the next a weary, wounded man, withdrawn, silent and grey.

Mugo, panting, buried his face in the cool, damp grass. His legs ached and trembled from the climb, and his clothes clung to him wetly. For a few moments he forgot Joshua, he forgot the forest behind and above them, and Mwengo. He even forgot his longing to be home, as he gave himself up to the relief of resting again. At last he rolled over, looking

85

back at his uncle who sat silhouetted against the late afternoon sky, still and tense.

"What do we do?"

"We go into the forest."

Mugo sat up to look at the densely growing trees, and as
though guessing his thoughts, Joshua said,

"We have to risk Mwengo."

Mugo almost told him then what he knew of his plans, but
he hesitated, not knowing what Joshua's reaction to that
might be. But he could not conceal his fear of the forest.

"There's nothing to be afraid of," Joshua went on,
noticing Mugo's anxiety. "You can trust me to get us
through without danger. And once we're over the mountain
— well, Nairobi won't be far." In spite of his encouraging
words, he gasped then with pain, and clutched at his leg
with both hands.

Mugo looked at him steadily, almost coolly, beginning to
understand the full nature of Joshua and his duplicity.

"I know what you are planning," he said quietly.

"Planning? I've just told you what I'm planning ... "

"You speak no truth. I was awake in the hut last night.
You sent a message to Mwengo. You said you wanted to
join him again." Mugo stopped speaking, afraid of what his
uncle might do. Joshua's face took on a terrible look of
suspicion and hate.

"You were listening? And my instinct didn't warn me?"
He staggered to his feet, standing to face the peaks of Mount
Kere-Nyaga. "I hope it isn't a bad omen. I hope you're not
bad luck for me ... It wasn't prophesied so. It cannot be so
... surely I would have felt it ... Ngai is not deserting
me ... " He turned fiercely on Mugo. "Boy, understand
this. Don't try to interfere with my plans. Understand that

if I didn't need your help because of this," he gestured to his leg, "I would have left you behind long ago. It would be as nothing to me to strangle you and throw you to the hyenas."

Nervously, Mugo clutched his bundle, his hand feeling for the comfort of the Decider, but Joshua's fierceness faded.

"You can believe this. We go into the forest, but we do not stay there. And we don't go yet. Mwengo knows I am coming. His men will be looking for me. Mwengo is treacherous, but Joshua is cunning." He smiled to himself. "Now I am coming home, boy. You'll have to learn from me about the forest, about my home." He became for the first time almost friendly to Mugo. "So, in a moment we will hide ourselves in those bushes higher up. And then we wait there for an hour at least, watching the forest to make sure no one is waiting for us. Remember that, boy. In the forest you can never spend too much time just watching ... "

## 12

IT was a rainy evening when they entered the forest. They were enclosed by the dense and awesome trees, their feet quickly clogged by the wet mud of the track they followed. As the big trees of the forest blackened out the twilight sky, Mugo shivered, his senses alive to the heavy, damp and threatening silence.

They seemed to be following some narrow animal track, and as they went deeper and it grew darker Mugo could not see anything and was guided in his stumbling climb only by the sound of his uncle's footsteps and breathing ahead of him, and he had to strain his ears even to hear that. His uncle was no longer the blind man. He moved with the swiftness and silence of an animal in its own environment.

"Uncle Joshua," said Mugo at last. He had stopped, exhausted, and because he could no longer hear his uncle. "Uncle Joshua."

"Ssh!"

They stood still. At first Mugo heard nothing but a series of rustlings, twitterings and squeaks, then suddenly out of the darkness came roars and cries that seemed to fade and grow nearer. He stumbled forward, bumped into his uncle and grabbed him.

"What is it? Let's get out—let's go back!" he cried.

"Shut up!" his uncle hissed. "There is a rhino about

fifty yards away. Do you want him to come charging us?"

"A rhino? How do you know?"

"There is also a storm coming up. Now you must follow me—and don't speak."

They went on, climbing through the thick and noisy darkness. Mugo was certain that at any moment he would be killed by some animal, bitten by a snake or captured by forest fighters. He could see nothing, but he could hear the increasing roar of wind in the tops of the trees.

Then his uncle stopped, and Mugo again ran right into him.

"Boy, you are clumsy."

Mugo said nothing. He was engulfed by a feeling of dreadful panic, as anyone would be if they had suddenly been struck blind and put into a maze full of wild beasts. And that was how Mugo felt, only for him the most dangerous and untrustworthy beast was the man he was relying on. Then through his panic came the voice of his father giving him the elders' decision that he should go with Joshua to Mombasa, and his father's voice again insisting that the journey was necessary, the testing was necessary to prove his grandmother's prophecy. Mugo got control of his panic. At least Joshua would not know of his fear. At least he would show Joshua he could also hold his tongue.

"A few yards ahead," whispered Joshua, "is a camp the forest fighters built. It was abandoned long ago, but we must approach very carefully even so. You stay here, till I call you."

Mugo began to protest, but this was useless. His uncle had gone. He stood there, afraid to move or to speak, for what seemed to him several years. Then he heard his uncle's voice close by him again, and felt his hand on his arm. They scrambled up a steeper slope on to level ground, walked a little distance and then seemed enclosed in an even deeper blackness, with the sound of the wind smothered. It was less cold. Mugo, already becoming accustomed to relying on his ears and his other senses rather than his eyes, realized that they were sheltered from the cold wind and the heavy, scattered drops of rain.

In a moment, there was a scraping sound, and light flared from a match. Above it his uncle's face hovered, lit weirdly from below, with the eyes large and wild. They were in a hut of bamboo and leaves, Mugo saw, a small round hut, with a narrow entrance. On the floor of beaten earth was the remains of a long-dead fire. Then the match went out.

"I am going to get firewood from the store if it is still there. Wait here."

This time his uncle returned quickly with a bundle of twigs. He struck another match and soon a small fire was leaping at their feet. Mugo crouched down beside it, holding out his cold hands to the blaze.

"We'll be safe here, at least for one night." Joshua threw more wood on to the fire, and sat down, leaning his back against the wall. He closed his eyes, and seemed to fall immediately into a deep sleep. Mugo studied him in the uncertain light. His face was so thin, and so full of shadows, with lines of pain down by the mouth and on the forehead, his wounded eye still swollen. Mugo noticed the bloodstain again on the trouser leg that was stretched out and that twitched now and then as though he felt pain even in his sleep. His shoes were heavy with mud. And from his uncle, Mugo looked round the small hut, and down at his own clogged shoes—the new shoes his beautiful sister had bought him—and the mud and scratches on his legs and arms. Thinking of the situation he was in, Mugo gave a slight groan of desperation. Immediately, his uncle was on his feet.

"What was that?"

"Only me."

"No noise, you tick," Joshua snarled. He looked round with a kind of wild weariness, then dropped back on to the ground and slept again.

Mugo sat looking at him for some moments in the fire-light. Rough and dangerous. Like Njangu. Total exhaustion, the weakness of hunger, the aching of his body, put the problem of Joshua and his own situation to the back of his mind. He took his jacket from his bundle and put it on, wrapped his blanket round him and, clutching the Decider in one hand and the money in the other, he fell asleep.

## 13

IN the shadowy hut the next morning, Mugo lay for several moments in alarm before he realized where he was. His uncle was stretched out like a dead man with the small fire at his feet from which came a wisp of flame. It was chill and damp. Mugo shivered, pulling his blanket round himself.

The hut gave him an eerie feeling because, in spite of its abandoned appearance, there were signs that someone had lived there quite recently. An old pot, some well-chewed bones, a skin bag and two rusty bully-beef tins that seemed to have been used as cups lay in a corner. Mugo regarded them anxiously, wondering whether they were valuable enough to their owner for him to come back for them. It was a bit like being in the den of an animal and waiting for its return.

The camp was built on a shelf in the hillside and, in the early light of morning that came uncertainly and coolly through the trees, the small plateau was steeped in silence. Mugo was stiff with the travelling and the rain of the previous day, and it was a relief to get out of the hut and into a warm shaft of sunlight. The camp, he thought, must have been bombed by the army when they were hunting the forest fighters and that must have made them abandon it. There was a huge crater at one side, and some trees were bent to the ground, shredded by the blast. Only three huts remained standing, and one of these leaned drunkenly. Round the edges of the plateau, the leaves had not yet begun to grow again on the branches that had been stripped bare.

In spite of the peacefulness of the forest just then, Mugo did not feel easy. For him it was the home of Mwengo, and Mwengo must know they were there. His men might be watching them at that moment, and the silence became sinister. Two huge and barbarically painted butterflies that swept past had the menace of spirits; when small deer frisked among the trees he watched for any sign that they were disturbed; and when birds called from the high branches above, he wondered whether they were bird-calls or the signals of the forest fighters. Mugo went a little way beyond the camp to collect firewood, searching for it under dead leaves so that it would be dry, and the fire in the hut soon burst into life. He was very hungry.

"Who is that?"

His uncle was awake, his eyes feverishly bright in the light of the fire.

"It's me—Mugo."

His uncle lay back with a groan, and Mugo realized that he would not be able to travel that day.

"We need food and water," Mugo said. "Give me your simi. Perhaps I can kill something with it."

Joshua looked round the hut with wary, bloodshot eyes. "Somebody's been here recently," he muttered. He thought for a while, then said, "Listen to me. There are three huts still standing—this one, the council chamber and the kitchen. The kitchen is towards the west and the stream is just beyond it. Behind the kitchen, under the fallen bamboo clump, there's a storage pit for food. If the animals haven't dug it up, there'll be something for us to eat."

Mugo found the pit, or what was left of it. The animals had left empty tins and skin bags scattered about, but no food except a tin half full of maize. Disappointed, Mugo carried this back to Joshua, who looked at it expressionlessly. He sat up, moistening his dried, grey lips with his tongue.

"Behind this hut," he said, "—thicket of thabai—a nettle we can eat. Be careful—it stings badly. Lift the top leaves away with a stick, and cut from underneath with my simi here. Not the top leaves—we don't want people to know we're here … "

Mugo managed to cut some of the nettle without getting stung, and took it back to the hut. Joshua nodded, looking at the stack of cut nettles.

"In that pot, we can make a stew with the nettle and maize," Joshua gasped, "but first, get some water. I must drink. My leg must be bathed … "

He writhed with pain, then snapped, "Go on, boy!"

Mugo turned to go, but his uncle called him back. "In case of danger—we must have a signal. The call of the nightjar will mean there are enemies about and one must not hesitate—one must run. Do you understand?"

Mugo nodded, and his uncle imitated the call of the nightjar—two trills and a plaintive whistle—and made Mugo repeat it to him.

"All right," he gasped, lying down again. "Now get me water."

Passing the council chamber, a bamboo shelter that was now only a few ant-eaten poles and some tattered hangings of thatch, Mugo saw inside rows of collapsing benches and a table. Under the table, he found a Challenge notebook, like the ones he used at school, damp and stained with water, and written on the front the title, "Battle History of the Camp", but the pages were so stained, Mugo could decipher none of the history.

The cookhouse was really just a shelter, for it had no walls, but there was a properly built fireplace, an overturned table and some gourds. Mugo picked up a gourd and went a little way into the forest to the stream.

As he bent down, holding a gourd in the clear water, he had a sudden sense of being watched, and looked up quickly. Across the stream stood the wild figures of some forest fighters, their hair in tight plaits, animal skins on their bodies and guns in their hands pointing straight at Mugo. Mugo dropped the gourd and it fell with a dull plop on the water and floated away downstream, turning round and round gaily like a dancer.

Mugo froze into stillness, his eyes on the fearsome group before him.

"Be quiet, boy, if you want to live."

Mugo did not move. He continued to gaze at the men. He wondered how he could warn his uncle.

They crossed the stream swiftly and silently and stood round him. The strong smell of the forest fighters in their clothes of animal skin encompassed him.

Mugo shivered, looking round from one fierce face to another, the bloodshot eyes, the mops of plaited hair, the skin jackets and the guns. It was only by will-power that he prevented himself from fainting.

"Where's your uncle?"

It was the question he'd been waiting for, but when it came it shocked him even more than their sudden appearance. He twisted to look up into the face of the man who'd spoken. The forest fighter had put a rough and calloused hand with a cheap ruby ring on it on Mugo's shoulder. His face was dark, his hair a dishevelled mop, but surely the voice was that of C.I. Mackenzie?

Could it be that under the mop of hair were the stern, European features, suitably darkened over, of the Chief Inspector?

"Do not keep us waiting, boy! Answer the C.I. promptly!"

And do your duty diligently *and* scientifically. The words fled through Mugo's mind. Surely that was the Homeguard in a coat made from the long, beautiful hair of the colobus monkey? Mugo felt dizzy. It was a horrible nightmare.

"We know your uncle is with you, boy. We've tracked you this far," said the Homeguard.

Still Mugo neither moved nor spoke, wondering why they had gone to so much trouble to disguise themselves simply to follow his uncle and himself into the forest. But it was Joshua they wanted, and he must prevent them from finding him. Mugo shrugged his shoulders as though giving in. He turned away as though leading them to Joshua, but instead of going towards the plateau, he moved downstream, following a narrow track, with the C.I. and the Homeguard and two policemen following him. He wondered how far they would go before they suspected what he was up to.

"You are not playing any tricks on us, are you?" asked the Homeguard at last, growing suspicious. "Where is your uncle? He cannot escape us."

At that, Mugo turned round, and, as he had arranged with his uncle, he gave the warning signal, the call of the nightjar—two trills and a plaintive whistle.

The men with him stopped short.

"He's warning his uncle," shouted the Homeguard and the C.I. grasped Mugo by the shoulder. "You must take us to your uncle. You can trust us. Do you understand?"

But Mugo, after his experiences with Joshua, did not trust anybody. He gazed back at the C.I. with blank, dark eyes, and hoped his uncle had had time to get away.

"You fool!" exclaimed the Homeguard.

"He doesn't understand," said the C.I. "I suspect we should have gone upstream."

Mugo watched cynically while they searched the camp. The fire in the hut told them that Joshua had been there, but he was not there now.

The Homeguard stood before him and Mugo noticed that his shoe still gaped thirstily. He pointed a long finger at Mugo. "Do you know the penalties for helping a dangerous criminal to escape?" he demanded. "You will be a jailbird for the rest of your life, and then who's going to marry those sisters of yours? Who is going to marry into a jailbird's family?"

Mugo shrugged and he retorted, "Who do you think is going to marry a homeguard?"

The Homeguard turned purple with rage.

"This boy must be jailed!" he cried. "C.I. Mackenzie! This boy is a hardened criminal!"

C.I. Mackenzie, who looked so odd in his forest fighter's disguise that Mugo, in spite of fear, wanted to laugh, came over to them.

"Leave him with me," he said. "I'll explain matters to him."

"It is better for me to question him. You don't know this

G

boy. He comes from a bad family—all his family—they are all bad!"

"That's a lie," exclaimed Mugo, "my father and grand-father are good men."

"Homeguard," said C.I. Mackenzie quickly, "I'll take over here. I want you to report back to base. Tell the rest of the men to be ready to move out at a moment's notice."

"But, C.I. ..."

"That is an order, Homeguard!"

The Homeguard snapped to attention, and Mugo smiled scornfully to himself as he watched him march smartly into the jungle. Then he turned to face C.I. Mackenzie.

He looked firmly up into his face. "You can torture me," he said, "but I will not tell you where my uncle is."

But the C.I. only put his hand on Mugo's shoulder, and looked inquiringly into his face.

"Boy," he said, "what do you know of your uncle's plans?"

"Nothing!"

"But you know", said the C.I. carefully, "that he came into the forest to escape us, and that he is now hiding from us."

"Yes."

The C.I. nodded. "And you", he said, "are simply trying to help him to escape from us? In that case, you know nothing and can't help us."

He looked round at the forest that was already pressing its way with silently moving undergrowth into the camp clearing. "So, he's out there somewhere, waiting for us to go. But listen, Mugo, if your uncle knew I was here, he would want to speak to me. You don't believe that? Yet it's true. Anyway, you can give him a message. Tell him I will wait in the cave of the Dorobo for the next two days if he wants to see me."

Mugo stared back at him with round eyes. What *was* he talking about?

"But what about you?" went on the C.I. "What will you do if Joshua doesn't return?"

Nothing of the shock Mugo felt at this suggestion showed in his face. He must show nothing of what he felt to this man. And so he stood still and expressionless, gazing at the C.I. He will come back, he thought, and then he remembered what Joshua had said to his father, that he would abandon Mugo if necessary.

The C.I. put his hand again on Mugo's shoulder.

"You are loyal to him, and you think he will be loyal to you," he said kindly, "but he might not. He's a tricky customer, twisted and cruel. This is the man we have an agreement with." Mugo began to protest, but the C.I. went on. "Look, Mugo, if your uncle does not return before evening don't go wandering about in the forest. Remember what I said and come to the cave of the Dorobo. Just follow the stream downhill until you come to a place where the stream goes underground. The cave is near there. It is not far away. Get there before darkness and I'll see you're taken safely out of the forest and sent home."

The C.I. then collected his men together and disappeared among the trees, leaving Mugo alone in the deserted camp.

Mugo did not give himself time to think about the C.I.'s words or the safety that had been so temptingly promised him. Instead he built up the fire again, filled the pot with water and put in the nettles and the maize.

The soup wouldn't be very satisfying stuff, but at least it was better than nothing. He crouched over the fire on his

99

haunches, gazing at the bubbling greenish liquid, his mind going over all that had happened. He thought Joshua would come back. His wounded leg made Mugo's help necessary to him, and in any case, his business in the forest hadn't been completed, Mugo was sure. Joshua had tricked them all at home. In his heart, Mugo acknowledged now that what the C.I. said had been true. Joshua would have wanted to speak to him. Yes, there was a connection between Joshua and the police, some arrangement between them, and Joshua had lied to the villagers when he said he had to escape both the police and Mwengo. He might have wanted to escape the police, but he had in fact made some kind of bargain with them so that although they watched him from the helicopter they did not try to arrest him.

Mugo stirred his nettle soup slowly, concentrating on his cooking so as not to think too closely about these things or about his loneliness in the jungle.

A hand grasped him suddenly by the shoulder and whirled him round, and he gazed into the face of Joshua that gleamed with beaded sweat.

# 14

"WHAT happened? Who was it?"

Joshua was scratched from his journey through the forest. His face was twisted with pain, and the sweat trickled through his growth of bristling, black beard.

"It was the police—C.I. Mackenzie and the Homeguard. They were disguised as forest fighters and I thought it was Mwengo and his men—that's why I warned you ... "

His uncle wiped a hand across his brow.

"Where are they now? What did you tell them?"

"Nothing. They've gone."

"But where to?" demanded Joshua, impatiently. "They must have left a message."

"Yes." Mugo spoke slowly. So his uncle *had* been expecting the police to arrive. "You wanted to see them—C.I. Mackenzie said so, but I didn't believe him."

Joshua was carrying the skin bag they had found in the hut, but now it was half full of some kind of liquid. He hung it carefully from a projecting nail and then helped himself to water. He drank so greedily from the calabash that the water dribbled down his chin and soaked into his shirt. His eyes had a wild, glazed look, and he looked to Mugo almost insane.

"What did Mackenzie say?"

Mugo repeated the message. Joshua listened without

comment, and Mugo said nothing. He poured out two gourds of soup and handed one to Joshua. He watched Joshua covertly all the time they drank, as he would have watched a wounded animal if he had had to share its lair, but Joshua turned on him at last.

"Why are you watching me, eh?"

He finished the soup and dropped the gourd on the ground.

"I said you would be necessary to me. My instinct ... Go and get some fresh water. My leg ... must be bathed ... " And he crawled away back into the hut, dragging his injured leg.

Mugo let out a cry of revulsion as, coming back with the water, he saw his uncle's unbandaged leg a mass of writhing, twisting maggots. Joshua's face was a still mask of pain, and he whimpered between his teeth as Mugo poured water over his leg. The maggots were washed away, leaving the leg raw. Joshua leaned back, exhausted. Then, his eyes, wild with fever, were turned on Mugo. He gestured to the skin bag.

"The bag—I collected honey in it. Honey and water—it will bring my strength back."

Mugo mixed honey and water in a gourd for him and having drunk, Joshua sank back on the ground, his eyes shut. He muttered and turned about restlessly, though he seemed asleep. Mugo sat looking at him. Joshua seemed mad, and he was certainly not able to walk. They would be forced to stay in the forest until his wound healed at least a little. But they couldn't survive long on nettle soup. Watching the uneasily sleeping figure, Mugo tried to make plans for venturing into the forest and shooting some animal. But the sound of the shots might attract Mwengo's men. Mugo looked down at his own muddied body and torn clothes. His legs and feet were swollen and ached. He was being overcome by a strange listlessness, and his mind did not seem to work very clearly. How long was it since he'd left home? One day? Two days? It seemed like a month. And why was he in this plight? For the sake of a treacherous, cunning man, the descendant of Njangu?

Joshua opened his eyes. He looked round like someone in a daze and then focused on Mugo. For a while he stared at him. Then he said, "You must go and find Mwengo's message."

"No," said Mugo.

Joshua stared at him.

"What are you saying? Go. I tell you to … "

"No." Mugo tried to appear calm and decided. He saw Joshua's hand moving in the direction of his belt where his *simi* was kept, and burst out, in desperation, "I'm not sure what you're up to, but I'm sure it's evil. You're cunning and a deceiver—and I won't help you!"

Joshua looked away and said nothing.

"My grandmother was right. You have the evil of Njangu in your blood!"

Joshua's lips curved contemptuously. "That old witch!" he muttered. After a while he turned to Mugo, pleadingly. "Nephew," he said, "you misjudge me. Believe me, what I'm asking is necessary."

Mugo hesitated. There was something disturbingly genuine about Joshua's voice and face.

"Look, man, I am sick and wounded. I can hardly move. And I am in greatest danger as long as that message of Mwengo's lies there. If it is not collected he will come seeking me. I speak the truth. I know Mwengo. He will seek out both of us."

Mugo looked searchingly into his uncle's face. Perhaps it was necessary to trust him ...

He was to cross the stream and then to keep it on his right— always on your right, Joshua had insisted. He would find a boulder shaped like a rhino's head, and then a clearing where there was a sacred fig-tree, a *mugumo*, with many white twisted roots like huge radishes dropping into the ground. Then he must stop, for he was near the valley where two waterfalls are heard at the same time. He must not go straight into the valley. That would be too dangerous. He must circle round it first, moving quietly through the forest, making sure there was no one about—no trap. Then he must go further on until he reached the first waterfall, and he must circle the valley again there. If he found nobody, he could go on to the valley where he would find the elephant's skull. He was to bring Mwengo's message back to Joshua.

Mugo, journeying alone through the forest for the first time, climbed the mountain, following the stream, throughout the heat of the afternoon, moving cautiously, trying to be as silent as his uncle. He knew the penalty if he was discovered by a forest fighter. He passed the rock shaped like a rhino's head, and he reached the sacred fig-tree. From there he circled the valley. There seemed to be no one about. He went on to the first waterfall and circled again. All seemed safe, and he entered the valley.

It was a small depression in the side of the vast mountain, and the tall forest trees towered above it, making it dim and cold on the floor of the valley where there was grass instead of undergrowth, and where his ears were filled with the splashing of the two waterfalls. He moved cautiously, until he was brought to a halt by a ghostly shape ahead. Something white and tall as a man was crouched before him, watching him from still, black eyes. Mugo gazed at it, unable to move, and then began cautiously to step backwards away from it. But the white presence did not move or make a sound, and gradually Mugo plucked up courage. He went slowly towards it, and realized with a shock of relief that it was the elephant's skull he had been looking for. Immediately, he dropped into the grass and lay still for an hour to make sure there was no one lying in wait for him. Then he wriggled forward like a snake to the skull and found inside, under a stone, a piece of paper folded.

To Joshua (it read):
    If the words brought to me by my followers from you speak the truth, we will meet by the tree of the dead honey-gatherer the day after you take this message. If your words are false, do not worry. Ngai will warn me of your treachery.
    It is I,                                          MWENGO

It took Mugo a long time to make his way back to the camp. Joshua had impressed on him that he must take every care to make sure he was not followed from the valley and that he left no tracks that could be followed. Where there was loose earth to be crossed, he walked on the side of his feet so as not to leave a track; he made sure that he did not break off twigs as he pushed through bushes; he did not even take a leaf from a branch. But going so carefully took time, and it was growing dark before he reached the camp and smelt the smoke from the fire.

Joshua was waiting for him. Although he still looked feverish and ill, he snatched the note from Mugo.

"How did you take so long? It's almost dark!" he exclaimed, and read the note quickly. For a moment he stood with his face upturned, as though listening. "You were not followed?"

Mugo sat down by the fire, shaking his head. His journey through the forest and the finding of Mwengo's note had only made more real and terrifying for him the presence of Mwengo. How could they hope to escape him? Surely he must already have marked them down. And when he discovered what Joshua was up to he would have no mercy. Mugo was certain now that his uncle was planning some treachery against Mwengo. It was not for nothing that the police had allowed him to re-enter the forest and were even then waiting to speak to him.

Joshua had sunk back on the ground, the note crumpled in his hand. He is too ill even for planning treachery, Mugo thought, and I am too exhausted to do anything about it. The strange feelings of exhaustion and fuzziness were worse after his journey through the forest. His legs and arms were bleeding, and his left hand had been bitten by some insect and was red and inflamed.

Too tired even to feel hungry, Mugo sipped some honey and water and slid into a heavy sleep.


He woke and sat up in the darkness, wondering where he was. The fire in the hut had sunk to a mere glow, and the wind outside moved round the hut, touching it like ghostly hands. In the distance he heard the howl of a hyena, and, shivering, remembered. The forest lay all round him, his home was far away. Mugo got up to throw more wood on the fire. As the flames licked the wood and leapt up, the

106

hut was fitfully lighted, and he saw that his uncle was not there.

Mugo cautiously crawled to the opening of the hut and looked out. The camp was quite still, but he was startled to see a glow of light in the centre of it. His thoughts turned at once to the spirits he had heard of that inhabited the forests, and as though to confirm his fears, from the glow of light came the sound of a voice. It rose and fell, as though talking to someone, but no one responded to it. Only the strange voice went on and on, and sometimes it broke into a burst of laughter.

Mugo had learnt enough of forest lore now, so that even if he had not been afraid he would not have gone straight to that hut. And now he moved cautiously round it, seeking a gap in the tattered walls which would let him see inside, while the hair on his scalp prickled.

Inside the hut there was only Joshua, leaning heavily against the swaying table in the light of a fire he had lit. His eyes glittered as he looked triumphantly round the empty hut with its ant-eaten benches, and addressed a ghostly audience of forest fighters. His words were only an unintelligible babble, though sometimes he stopped, his head on one side, to listen to some other imaginary speaker, and sometimes he nodded agreement, and sometimes he smiled and waved his *simi* about his head. On the floor at his feet lay the exercise book entitled "Battle History of the Camp", and round him pressed the dark silence of the forest.

"Uncle Joshua!" cried Mugo.

His uncle paused.

"Who is that? Is that Kamba speaking? Speak up General Kamba."

Mugo came forward into the light. His uncle's eyes were

turned glittering on him, but Mugo knew that in his delirium he didn't recognize him.

"It's time to end the meeting," said Mugo.

"Ah—the meal is ready? Come then, brothers. We must eat ... "

He swayed, and almost fell, but Mugo supported him, and together they stumbled back to the hut. Joshua sank to the ground, his *simi* still clutched in his hand, and Mugo sat by the fire, thinking that Joshua might die here in the forest. And then he would be on his own.

It was the longest night Mugo had ever known. He kept the fire going, and sat by Joshua, watching him anxiously, listening to his mutterings, bathing his forehead and wetting his dry lips with water from the stream. Once, most terrifyingly, Joshua had risen up from the ground again and stalked away from the camp into the darkness of the forest, and only by pretending to be a fighter with a message from Mwengo had Mugo been able to get him back to the camp. After that he lay quite still, like one who was dead.

As the light of morning crept through the clearing, Mugo woke from a short, uneasy doze, cramped and shivering. He got up to look at Joshua and could not tell whether he was alive or dead, he lay so still, hardly breathing at all, his lips dry and cracked, with a white rime on them. Mugo was relieved when he felt some breath from his mouth, and he built up the fire and went to find more nettles.

All morning Joshua lay in the hut and Mugo became more and more anxious. He began to think he should risk getting lost in the forest and go and seek out C.I. Mackenzie. After all anything was better than sitting there with a man in a coma.

But towards midday, Joshua stirred. His eyes opened, and he looked round blankly at Mugo. Mugo hastened to him and he drank some honey and water. He sat up, propped against the wall of the hut, a thin, dark skeleton. But Mugo thought he was better. His wounded leg looked cleaner and the fever had gone. He sat there with a cunning look on his face, and at times his eyes rolled in Mugo's direction, studying his face. Mugo, still feeling strangely weak and ill, sat in silence also, brooding over what was to happen to them.

Suddenly Joshua croaked,

"Did you take a message to Mwengo?"

Mugo was startled, realizing that in spite of being so ill, Joshua's brain never ceased to work on his problems and that even now he was turning over some plan in his mind.

"I brought the message from Mwengo," said Mugo, thinking Joshua had forgotten.

His uncle shook his head impatiently.

"You must take a message back," he croaked, "at the tree of the dead honey-gatherer. You know what his message was. I was to meet him at the tree of the dead honey-gatherer today. If I am not there and there is no message … " he shrugged. "If he thinks I'm tricking him, he will not rest till he has killed us."

Mugo looked with his dark eyes in blank distrust of Joshua. "*You* keep the appointment. I'll help you to get there."

Joshua shook his head impatiently. "You see how ill I am—how can I travel so far?"

And so, reluctantly, Mugo wrote out a message on a sheet of paper from his uncle's notebook:

To Mwengo:
    Joshua is sick because of his wound and cannot

travel to meet you. He will leave another message in the skull of the elephant when he is well.

It is I,            MUGO, NEPHEW OF JOSHUA

"When do you think", asked Mugo anxiously, "that you will be well enough to travel?"

Joshua shook his head impatiently. "The tree of the dead honey-gatherer is hollow at the bottom. It is used as a secret letter-box by Mwengo. Leave the message inside and it will be collected." And then he grinned and muttered, "He will be waiting for it!" He asked suddenly, "What have you done with our money?"

"I have it in my shirt pocket."

"Better leave it here. If you lose it—how do we finish our journey?"

Mugo queried, "Finish our journey?"

"Did you think I meant to stay with Mwengo?" Joshua spat. "I am too big to stay with Mwengo. No. I just have something to say to him. Then we go on."

There was some sense in his suggestion about the money. Slowly Mugo took the money and laid it beside his bundle on the floor of the hut.

"There's the Decider also," said Joshua. "I hope you've taken care of it."

"I told you. It is buried in my sisters' shamba."

"Your father said you would carry it … "

"My father said afterwards it was not safe for me to bring it. He took it from me."

"Then he lied!"

Mugo met Joshua's infuriated gaze with blank, concealing eyes. Joshua turned away, lying down again. "It is of no importance. We don't need it."

Carefully folding the note, Mugo asked thoughtfully, "You lived in this camp, didn't you?"

Joshua looked at him sharply. "This was my headquarters. I was in charge of all the south-east section of the forest. The best run section! Better than Mwengo's! His camp was dirty—there were no rules. Mine—mine was well ordered, my men well trained—I was a better leader than Mwengo. He was jealous of me. That's why he shot me. He feared me ..."

"I thought you said you accidentally shot him?"

Joshua looked withdrawn and contemptuous. "Everything ordered," he murmured. "Books properly kept, reports written, plans made ..." He looked up at Mugo. "You must get that message to Mwengo." His eyes glazed and he lay down, and Mugo stood watching as his eyes closed in weakness. But, "I don't trust him," he told himself, and as Joshua slipped into a heavy doze, Mugo took the Decider quietly from his bundle.


The tree of the dead honey-gatherer was higher up towards the bamboo belt than the valley of the two waterfalls. Mugo knew from his uncle's description, as soon as he saw the huge, straggling trees hundreds of feet high with the dark shapes of beehives in their branches, that he was reaching the place where the secret letter-box was. And soon he saw the tree with the bones of the dead honey-gatherer who had slipped and been strangled in the branches years before, still hanging there. A sudden wind tossed the upper branches and the legs of the skeleton stirred as though it was taking a light-hearted walk in the air.

He did not approach the tree openly. He was too wise for

that now. He crawled through the undergrowth, an inch at a time, trying not to leave a trail of trembling bushes behind him. At the foot of the tree he found the hollow and carefully placed the note inside. It was very quiet there. He didn't think there was anyone about, until a *ndete* bird appeared, hovering over a distant bush. The *ndete* bird is very sensitive to anything out of the ordinary. Mugo lay quite still. There was nothing to be seen or heard. Only the bird fluttered its alarm.

Then a high voice called from the bush,

"Stand, and name all those with you!"

Mugo could not be certain, but he felt this must be Mwengo. He stood up, trembling, gazing towards the bush, but he could not see anyone.

"I am alone," he replied, his voice a mere croak.

"Name yourself."

"I am Mugo, nephew of Joshua."

"Name those with you."

"I am alone," Mugo insisted.

"You lie, you tick! I am Mwengo. I have my gun pointing at you. Do not lie to me!"

Mugo licked his dry lips, and tried again. "I am alone. Joshua is sick and could not meet you. He sent me to leave a message for you. It is in the hollow in the tree of the dead honey-gatherer."

"Joshua is a cunning rat, and I do not trust him or any of his family. Come here, hyena, and move slowly. My soldiers are all watching you ... "

Mugo, desperately regretting he had agreed to deliver this message, began to move slowly forward through the thick bush. With his head and shoulders plainly visible, he felt very vulnerable. The bush from which Mwengo had spoken was at the top of a small hill. Mugo ascended it slowly, and he had almost reached the top when, looking up, he saw the face of Mwengo glaring at him over the bush. He had an impression of fierce, bloodshot eyes and long, black, plaited hair above a leopardskin coat, and then there was a deafening rattle of gunfire and the whole area echoed and flashed. Mugo dropped like a dead bird into the undergrowth and lay still.

In the momentary silence that followed, he clearly heard the voice of the Homeguard: "Come here, boy—Mugo, come here. It is the C.I.'s orders ... " and then the guns began again from both sides, and Mugo did not hesitate. He slithered away on all fours towards the stream and safety.

## 15

MUGO reached the stream and bathed the mud from his body. He had no recollection of getting away from the battle beside the tree of the dead honey-gatherer, and he went swiftly downstream towards the camp in a stiff and dream-like state. If he was quick enough, his mind told him as though from a long distance, his uncle might not have left.

But he had, as Mugo really knew he would. The camp was empty. Mugo began running about, crying silently, cursing his uncle for a cunning and treacherous rat, kicking aside the honey-bag, the remnants of the fire, the gourds, in a frenzy of hatred. When he stopped at last he sat down, exhausted, and the silence of the ruined camp pressed in upon him.

He had been a fool. In spite of knowing what Joshua was, knowing he was involved in some intrigue, knowing he could not be trusted, Mugo had trusted him. Because he could not believe that finally Joshua would betray him, a boy, his own nephew. But he had gone even that far. Joshua had made a bargain with the police to lead them to Mwengo—no doubt in return for his own freedom. So he arranged a meeting with Mwengo and told the C.I. where and when it was to be. Shaken, Mugo realized that immediately after he had left the camp to take his uncle's message, Joshua must have hurried away, in cold blood, to tell the

C.I. so that the police could follow Mugo. Joshua hoped Mwengo would be killed or captured, and for good measure, to get rid of Mugo, he put him right between the two lines of fire. He was a coward, a traitor—"Rhino! Hyena! Snake!" Mugo shouted to the empty camp, and sobbed again as he thought how near he had been to death.

But soon, remembering that he was now alone in the forest, he stopped crying. He had to make plans. His uncle had stolen his blanket and the money, but he still had the Decider. I'll find him, Mugo decided. I'll find him and kill him! His uncle would not stay in the forest longer than was necessary. Joshua could not be certain that Mwengo would not escape the ambush and come after him. But he would not be able to travel far at a time. Now that he had the money, would he not have gone south at once, out of the forest, where he could get a taxi to take him to Nairobi? But Mugo thought not. There would be friends of Mwengo searching for him when the news of the ambush filtered out. He would never be safe, and Joshua would know that. So he would have to travel north-east, towards the summit.

Mugo took a firm grip on the gun and started to look for tracks. And when he found them—the imprint of his uncle's shoes in the mud of an animal track leading up through the forest—he felt new energy and determination flow through him. He followed the track as swiftly as he could—he was the hunter now.


The track was so easy to follow that Mugo concluded that Joshua was feeling very safe. But eventually the forest gave way to the belt of bamboo where there were no tracks to be followed. Mugo decided he would go on climbing upwards until he reached the moorlands. If he didn't find his uncle, he would then be completely lost, but he had to take the risk. The bamboo was so thick at times that he had to crawl through pig tunnels, narrow and claustrophobic, where his skin was irritated by a powder of prickly hairs from the bamboo, and from which he would crawl out to pick leeches from his body. At other times he had to clamber over piles of fallen bamboo, and every movement of his swollen legs was painful; his body, weakened by lack of food, protested it could go no further, and his hand was swollen from the insect bite and still throbbed painfully. But he kept on climbing by telling himself how he would find his uncle. He no longer wished to kill him but at gun-point force him on to Nairobi—he would not be fooled by Joshua again! As he climbed on he began to wonder whether he could still be held to his promise to his father. To go on journeying with such a man as Joshua, didn't this make him, Mugo, a fool rather than a great leader as his grandmother had prophesied? But such thoughts didn't last long, for Mugo was urged on by strong anger against Joshua for his treachery and betrayal, and a determination to make him suffer for it. He went on stubbornly.

He stumbled out gratefully from the belt of bamboos, from the pale light under the interlocking branches into bright sunlight again, but sunlight that had the sharp, cold tang of the heights, and Mugo stopped, breathless and weary, but overpowered by what he saw. He was on top of the world, almost above the sun that was declining down the sky to the west, and looking down on valleys, forests and hills. The moorland, with its wet grasses, clumps of giant heather, higher than a man, rocks and ravines and trees bearded with long, grey creepers, was vast and silent. By the mud bank of a nearby stream he could clearly see the spoors of many animals and birds. It was so still and silent there. And far over to the east he could see the two pinnacles of Mount Kere-Nyaga, where Ngai lived. He felt very lonely and young.

Mugo hesitated on the verge of the moorlands, afraid to set off on the search for Joshua over that bleak and frightening stretch of land. If he was lost there, he would surely die of cold in the night. Again it came strongly to him that he should give up the search and go back through the forest. But the thought that he would be giving up his purpose and that he might anyway be equally lost in the forest stopped him. He walked over the marshy ground to a small hillock and climbed it to have a better view of the ground.

At first he could see nothing of interest, but then he caught sight of a faint spiral of smoke behind a huge clump of giant heather. It might not be his uncle's fire—it could be made by forest fighters. He would know very soon now.

As he got closer, the wind blew the scent of smoke and of roasting flesh towards him, and in spite of the danger, his mouth watered at the thought of roast meat. He drew the gun, and peered cautiously through the branches of heather. Crouched over the low, smouldering fire, his back towards him, was a man. Certainly it was his uncle. His hair was untidy and his long coat muddied and torn. It was Joshua.

Thrown off balance by finding him so soon, Mugo sat back to think out a plan. His uncle was stronger—he could not be forced to do anything. And his uncle was cunning—he could not be trusted. But he would finish the journey! With the gun gripped in both hands, Mugo crept up behind

117

the seated man and suddenly pressed the barrel into the back of Joshua's neck.

"Don't move," he muttered.

Joshua's head jerked back as if his neck had been caught in a wire snare, and his eyes turned wildly towards Mugo. As he recognized his nephew, a wide, frantic grin split his face.

"Mugo!" he gasped. "Eeei! Mugo!"

"Mugo." Mugo's voice was grim. He did not move. Indeed he was not sure what to do next, but he'd outwitted his uncle's strong instinct for danger.

"Be careful, boy. That gun—be careful with it. And why threaten me with it? I'm your uncle. A bullet has a home only in the belly of an enemy."

Mugo began to feel weak after the long climb through the forests, his swollen hand could not grip the gun well and he felt it shake in his hands. Let Joshua see that and it would all be over.

"The simi," he said, as firmly as he could. "Take the simi and throw it down there by the fire."

"The simi? The simi? Does it worry you? Well, well. You had only to say. There you are … "

The double-edged knife fell into the grasses and lay shining there. Mugo, keeping the gun pointed at Joshua, went cautiously to pick it up, and with a swift movement dropped it into a deep pool nearby. It was Joshua, not himself, who watched the blade's silvery path into darkness.

Joshua grunted. "Well, that was stupid, boy. We might need that simi yet."

"You meant me to be killed in that ambush."

Joshua sniggered and Mugo clutched the gun more firmly.

118

"You arranged for the police to ambush Mwengo at the tree of the dead honey-gatherer."

Joshua hesitated. "Mwengo was my enemy. I owed him my revenge. I'm greater than the great Mwengo! But you know, Mugo, I never thought the fighting would start so soon. You must believe that. I thought the police would have to wait hours, maybe days, before Mwengo appeared. He is so careful usually—I thought we would both be safely away. Then I heard shots in the distance. I thought there was no hope for you then."

"You never thought of coming to rescue me?"

"Rescue you? What hope was there of rescue from an ambush like that? How did *you* escape? You must have moved as quick as a lizard!"

Mugo's mind was more suspicious at the flattery in Joshua's voice.

"You stole my bundle with the money ... "

"Dead boys, like dead men, need no money ... Do you believe, Mugo, that your father's brother would wish you any harm?" He paused and then went on, "I see you had the Decider after all. That was cunning of you, Mugo. Where did you hide it?" There was no fear in Joshua.

He stirred the fire with a stick. "You must be hungry, Mugo. I found a dik-dik in a trap up here and it's ready for eating now. Sit down and eat."

Mugo hesitated. The smell of roast meat after so many days of near-starvation was a strong temptation.

"Come, sit. Eat. What have you to fear now?"

"I'll keep the Decider," said Mugo. "And when we've eaten, I'll tell you what we're going to do."

In his heart, Mugo had no idea what they were going to do. Holding the gun in his right hand, his eyes never leaving his uncle's face, he ate the roast meat as well as he could with the other. The light of the fire made a little flickering island of light in the vast cold of the moorlands, and seemed to distort his uncle's features so that now he seemed to smile and now to frown and now to grimace with pain. Getting Joshua to Mombasa would be like trying to drive a cunning animal from its lair, but he believed that he owed it to his family and his village to see that Joshua left the country. Yet how could he manage it? At any moment Joshua might slither away into the forest and disappear. He would leave Mugo lost in that wilderness, Mugo did not doubt that.

"My father risked his life to save you!" he burst out suddenly. "You are his kinsman. How can you be treacherous to his only son?"

Joshua looked steadily at him from under his brows through the light of the fire. His voice was slurred.

"You don't understand. You know nothing!"

"I know you left me to die."

Joshua gazed away into the darkness, the whites of his eyes flashing in the gloom, the light shining over the surfaces of his face. Mugo shivered. Always he felt that Joshua was alert with all his senses, listening, looking, feeling, knowing so much more of what was going on about them. The wind sighed in the giant heather and then blew strongly with a bitter chill from the distant summit.

"You may sit there with that gun in your hand, but it might as well be the stick you use for herding goats for all the good it will do you against me and the forest. The forest is my friend. It is your enemy."

Mugo knew these words were true. But still he grasped the gun more firmly. He would not give up without a struggle.

"Was Mwengo killed in the ambush?"

"How could I tell? I didn't stay, I got out fast!"

To Mugo's surprise, Joshua chuckled. His eyes glinted with amusement in the firelight. "You are learning to be a good forest fighter, Mugo! In a dangerous situation, you get out fast. That is a golden rule. Well, whatever has happened to Mwengo, I have fulfilled my part of the bargain."

"A bargain with the C.I.?"

There was no reply.

"You had made that bargain with the C.I. before you came to our village, hadn't you? You had agreed with him to draw Mwengo into a trap?"

Joshua continued to smile, his eyes gazing into the fire.

"I suppose you were captured when you came out of the forest wounded, and you agreed to sell Mwengo for your own freedom. And then you had to pretend to be running from the police so that the news got back to Mwengo and he would trust you enough to arrange a meeting? You didn't care about bringing trouble to our village, you didn't care about leading me into danger, you didn't care about treachery to your leader ... It is what my grandmother said, there is evil in the blood of our family ... "

Joshua looked up from the fire. "There is plenty of brushwood and heather about. Collect enough to cover yourself during the night. Unless you want to be dead of cold tomorrow."

## 16

SHIVERING under the heap of brushwood he had pulled over himself, and wrapped in his blanket which Joshua, with a sharp laugh, had returned to him with his money, Mugo slept fitfully. "He who is pinched knows how to defend himself," Joshua had said mockingly, meaning that Mugo would be more careful in future. After his uncle had plunged them into darkness by dousing the last of the fire with earth, he had been left in a cold, dark world.

Mugo's thoughts went round and round and round his dilemma, his mind too tired to deal with it, yet unable to forget it. Since Joshua had traded his own freedom for Mwengo's, surely he would want to leave the country quickly so that Mwengo's followers could not catch up with him. And he, Mugo, could say goodbye to that strange and treacherous man and return to his own village. His hand clutched the gun which he had insisted on keeping, and whenever he began to doze he would jerk awake again, desperately seeking for the Decider among the heap of brushwood. Towards morning he did sleep, but woke again soon, conscious that some light was penetrating the pile of undergrowth over him. He sat up, stiff and damp, afraid that Joshua would not be there.

He could see nothing. He was surrounded by a heavy

white mist through which there loomed only vague forms.

"Uncle Joshua!"

There was a stirring near him, and he vaguely saw a dark mound heave like a minor earthquake, then scatter and his uncle appear sitting in it.

"I am here."

Still sitting in their bundles of heather for the little warmth there was, they ate what was left of the roast meat. Then Joshua set about erasing all signs of their camp, and Mugo pushed the Decider into his belt, and fastened his coat to hide it. He looked hastily at Joshua and got the impression that he had been watching the fate of the gun. They started off over the moorlands, stumbling through a mist that sometimes cleared abruptly to reveal a stretch of glistening wet grass and still, cold pools, and sometimes descended as abruptly leaving them to feel their way forward. Joshua led the way, and Mugo, in spite of cold and weariness, forced himself to keep up with him, clutching his blanket round him. He could not imagine how Joshua kept on, or how he knew which way to go. But Joshua did not seem to hesitate, and he did not seem lost.

And then the mist cleared again, and he saw the sky fired gold and red over the distant peaks of Mount Kere-Nyaga and seeing the mountain of brightness, Joshua stopped and scooped up some earth with his left hand. Holding it to his breast, he raised his other hand to the mountain and cried, "Soil and peace! Freedom and peace! People and peace! Peace! Peace!" Then he turned to Mugo with a crooked but jubilant grin. "Now I've really gained something, eh?" And turning again to the mountain, he prayed, "O, Ngai! My thanks to you for bringing me prosperity—bringing it for me only, for Joshua!" He gave a strange laugh. "Come on, then. We mustn't trouble Ngai too much."

And they walked on through bright, cold sunshine, with a buzzard hanging overhead from a deep blue sky. The empty landscape stretched on and on, and his uncle was there ahead of him, a limping figure in a flapping coat, a kind of strange devil figure leading the way. So it had been at the beginning.

He stopped by a stream. "See this—the stream is flowing towards the south-east—downhill, to Nairobi. We're over the watershed."

As the day drew on, they reached the edge of the forest, the smell of heat came up to them from the plain, a dry dusty smell of earth and cattle and trees. They came out into the sunshine, on to a hillside sloping down to wider pastures, to patches of bracken and fern, to distant clusters of villages and there was the tinkle of goat bells again. Below them lay the yellow plain and further on the city. Mugo sank down on to the ground, overcome by weariness, his legs newly torn and bleeding from the journey through the forest, his body aching and his eyelids drooping sleepily under the influence of the sun.

"I will never", he vowed, "go into the forest again." But he felt safer. Even if Joshua left him now, he could find his way home. He was free of the forest.

He was startled by a strange guttural sound, and turning, realized it was Joshua laughing. He gazed down in the direction of the city, shaking with a deep, quiet laughter.

"Now my life begins," he said. "A new life—freedom, a new life—wealth!" He chanted the words, with his head thrown back.

"It hasn't begun yet," said Mugo drily, from where he sat at Joshua's feet. "There's Mwengo's followers."

"Who was the most cunning man in the forest? Who was the swiftest runner, the most skilful general? Not Mwengo. Not his followers. Me. I should have been leader. But none of them can defeat me—now or later. Listen, Mugo. I am no fool. It was not only my freedom I bought with Mwengo. Read!"

He thrust a piece of paper into Mugo's hand. It was written in English, in a neat handwriting. It told whoever read the note to give safe conduct to Joshua and to take him to C.I. Mackenzie.

"You see, Mugo? I will get freedom and money for Mwengo. The price on Mwengo's head is high, and it is mine. Joshua is a rich man, Mugo. A rich man."

Mugo looked away from Joshua's jubilant face. In his heart he kept his own decisions—to watch Joshua as he would a poisonous snake, and to see him on to a ship at Mombasa. With the first idea in mind, he deliberately folded up his blanket and placing the Decider in the centre of the long strip, rolled it up carefully and tied it with a strip of *muondee*, the forest string. Joshua watched him closely.

"You're keeping the Decider? You don't trust me. Mugo is very wise." He laughed again. "We'd better try to tidy ourselves up a bit, eh? For going into the city."

He had never been so talkative before, and Mugo felt irritated by him. He would rather, he thought, have the silent Joshua. He no longer was afraid of this strange man with blood of Njangu in his veins, he was only suspicious of him, distrustful. You could never trust Joshua.

They washed in a stream, tidied their hair, brushed down

their clothes—but they could do little to hide the tears and stains from the jungle or the scratches and weals it had left on their skin. His body more weary and stiff than before, Mugo turned his face to the warmth of the sun in thankfulness, at least, that he had left the jungle.

"I am ready," he said, and started down the hillside towards the city. Joshua, grinning to himself, followed with a long, loping stride.

They came into the city by a winding road from the hills above, mingling with the early morning crowd of women bringing food to the markets, and bent under the weight of bundles hung by straps from their foreheads.

They reached a row of barbers, each with his big wooden chair with a wooden canopy set on the pavement. With a sign to Mugo to wait, Joshua approached one of these men and said something quietly to him. Mugo recognized at once from the man's fear and deference that he knew who Joshua was, and Joshua sat in the chair and the man shaved him, all the time making polite conversation and telling him what he knew of the rumours in the city. Mugo crouched before them, his bundle by his side, watching Joshua with a smouldering sullenness of anger. This man who had betrayed his companions, brought danger to his family, cheated and lied—why, it looked as though he was going to be rich and happy and free. It was not right, Mugo thought. It was not right.

Joshua strode along quite indefatigable now, in front of Mugo, and Mugo had to walk quickly to keep up with him and not get lost in the crowd. It irritated Mugo. Without any explanation Joshua had suddenly ceased to limp so badly. He had borrowed a couple of shillings from Mugo to buy a wide-brimmed felt hat from a stall on the outskirts of the city and he wore it pulled down over his face with his sun-glasses beneath it. He had taken off the long overcoat and carried it over his arm. He held his head up and walked firmly and confidently. Mugo, with nothing left of his bundle now but a rolled up blanket and the Decider, caught up with him.

"You are no longer a blind man."

"There is no need for that disguise now. Besides, the police and Mwengo's followers will be looking for a blind man and a boy. It is better for you to walk behind."

Mugo was very angry.

"Now walk behind me I say, and don't attract attention."

The crowds, the traffic, the strange buildings and the shops full of foreign goods were things Mugo had never seen before, and he was constantly tempted to stop, but when he did this once he found he'd completely lost sight of Joshua. To be lost in this city seemed to be almost as dangerous as being lost in the forest. Joshua dodged across roads with scarcely a glance, hopping in and out and round about the traffic, ignoring shouts and hoots and the ring of bicycle bells, and Mugo was forced to leap off the pavement after him. Joshua led the way to a small covered market, crammed with wooden stalls selling everything from cheap, bright cotton clothes to dried fish. One corner was given over to a small eating-place where, in front of several square wooden tables, a cook, in a cloud of steam, kept the corn-cakes sizzling on a pan.

"First," said Joshua, jubilantly, "we eat. Then I collect the money. Blood money,"—he spoke proudly. "Then I take you to your aunt and she'll send you back home."

"That's not the arrangement," said Mugo stubbornly.

"The arrangement is finished. In an hour or two I am a

127

free man and I am a rich man. Then what do I do? I'll tell you. Until all of Mwengo's followers are picked up, I'm still in danger. All right. I'll fly out of here. Yes, man, I'll fly! And when the trouble's over, and I've seen a bit of the world, I'll fly back." He surveyed the small eating-place. "And one of these days I'll lead this country!"

Mugo had no faith in such wild dreams, but he had learnt enough to keep his eyes open where Joshua was concerned. He sat eating the meal which Joshua had paid for out of their small store of money, and tried to remember when he had last eaten a proper meal and how many days it had been since he left home. What would they be thinking in the village? Joshua ate quickly, his eyes alert for everybody in the café. Then he bought a cheroot and sat back on the wooden stool smoking and, Mugo was sure, imagining himself a rich man. Could a man really thrive on such treachery? If Joshua could become a rich man out of betraying Mwengo, might he not also one day become one of the country's leaders? Eating the last of his corn-cakes, Mugo wondered whether his grandmother had been wrong. Perhaps the evil in family blood was what made great men.

Beside him at the table sat a very old man with stooped shoulders and a head of wiry grey hair. His eyes studied Joshua's face again and again over his plate of stew. Mugo began to have a sensation of uneasiness. No doubt the old man was harmless, as were that group at the next table gambling with an old pack of cards and raising a shout of triumph every now and then. A pedlar of watches came to their table, rolling up each sleeve in turn to show the watches strapped to each arm, twisting them about to let the light shine on their glass and chrome. And then Mugo saw Joshua become alert, stiffen, wave the pedlar away. But the

128

man would not go. He put his hand into his pocket and pulled out a packet of photographs.

"Buy a photograph then? Photograph of our great leader in the forest?"

Mwengo's face, staring out at them from a photograph on the table, startled both of them. Mugo knew his uncle would take it as a bad omen, and indeed Joshua was glaring down at the face of his enemy as though hypnotized. "No, no!" he muttered, waving his hand.

"Mwengo's great lieutenant, then, Joshua ... "

Joshua's stool scraped on the floor as he pushed it back. The sight of his own face next to Mwengo's was too much for him.

"These are new photographs—very popular. Very secret."

It was Mugo who tried to cover up Joshua's panic.

"We are very poor ... "

"These are very cheap ones for you!"

"And very dangerous photographs also," the old man beside him said. "Jail for you, man, if they find you selling them."

The pedlar hastily swept the photographs out of sight. "I was not selling to you!" he retorted.

"Joshua's is most dangerous of all, maybe. Have you heard the news from the forest?" The old man looked round at their faces. "Mwengo is dead." The pedlar cried out, but Mugo, watching Joshua, saw his face become blank, watched him pull his hat lower over his brow and put on his dark glasses casually.

"Yes, dead. Killed in ambush."

"This is terrible news."

"How do you know this?" demanded Joshua.

"I know these things," the old man nodded. "And I

I

know more. Joshua betrayed Mwengo. Yes, Joshua. They will be hunting Joshua everywhere ... " His eyes were fixed on Joshua's face, and with the swift movement of the iguana, Joshua had left the table and was half out of the eating-place.

# 17

IT took Mugo all his time to keep Joshua in sight as he went swiftly through the busy streets of the city. Still carrying his depleted bundle, Mugo ran after him, dodging people and traffic, afraid to call his name in case of attracting attention.

He almost ran into Joshua at last, where he had stopped under the trees lining a busy road to stare at a building opposite. Mugo felt Joshua was again in the forest, alert, suspicious, looking over the ground before he made a move.

Wearily Mugo put his bundle down and sat on it.

He was tired of all this chasing about. What was Joshua up to? Joshua had taken a piece of paper from his pocket and was smoothing it out with nervous fingers. He handed it to Mugo, who saw it was the note from C.I. Mackenzie giving Joshua safe passage, and handed it back.

"That is the police station opposite," said Joshua, his eyes carefully noting the cars and the Jeep drawn up before it, the white and black policemen who came and went. "I am going in there to collect my reward."

"It looks very busy," said Mugo, with some sarcasm. "Do you think they'll have time for you?"

"You tick! Have you learnt nothing yet?" It was the old Joshua speaking. "Yes, it is busy. And that makes me suspicious." He threw his head back, his eyes, ears and nose all busy, his instincts centred on the station. "Something has happened."

"You've got your note from the C.I. You're safe."

"Something is wrong."

Mugo stood up. "All right," he said. "I'll try to find out what's happening. It's safer for me." He crossed the road, carrying his bundle, and Joshua did not stop him. The busy policemen took no notice of the ragged boy who loitered before the station, apart from brushing him out of their path, and nobody spoke to him when he stopped before the poster on the notice board and stood reading it. The very sight of it sent a chill of fear down his spine. It was Joshua's face on the poster, with the word WANTED above it, and below, FOR THE MURDER OF C.I. MACKENZIE, KILLED IN AMBUSH.

Mugo walked on down the street. He made himself walk slowly, though he wanted to run. On the opposite side walked Joshua, also casually. At the next junction, Mugo crossed the road, and Joshua, his instinct warning him of disaster, dragged him round the corner.

"What is it?"

"C.I. Mackenzie is dead. He died in the ambush."

Joshua's face did not change. He stared ahead at the traffic, unseeingly.

"They think you arranged to have him killed—they want you for murder."

Still Joshua said nothing.

"You better go straight away and explain things and show them the C.I.'s note. Otherwise, somebody might recognize you and shoot you down in the street." Mugo paused. "The C.I. was a good man, I think," he said regretfully. "He was kind to me in the forest." He looked at Joshua again.

"Go on—claim your reward. Enough men have died for it."

He was amazed to see Joshua tearing the C.I.'s note into shreds. His face was twisted and bitter. "There'll be no money," he said quietly. "It has all been for nothing." The shreds of paper fell to the ground.

"The reward's still yours," protested Mugo. "You helped to trap Mwengo—it wasn't your fault the C.I. died. But without that note … "

"The note's useless. My arrangement with Mackenzie was private. It was between the two of us. Nobody else could be told. Nobody—in case the plan leaked out and was carried to Mwengo. Only Mackenzie knew I helped him trap Mwengo—and Mackenzie is dead."

To the passers-by they were just a boy and a man talking on the pavement, a scratched and ragged boy with a bundle, maybe begging money from the man in the straw trilby and sun-glasses with the coat over his arm.

"All for nothing!" muttered Joshua. He stood like one stunned, his shoulders drooping, unable to move. "It was a bad omen. The photograph was a bad omen. I knew it … This city is a trap … "

And it was. Mugo knew it. The police wanted Joshua for killing the C.I., and when the people learnt he had betrayed their leader, there wouldn't be a place in the city where he could safely hide, not a person he could trust.

"My aunt lives in Kabete," Mugo insisted. "She is nurse-maid to a European family there. You remember my father told us. Do you know where Kabete is?"

"Kabete?"

"You must take me there! She can give us money for the

133

train to Mombasa and shelter until it is time to leave. She is the only one we can trust."

Joshua walked slowly, like a man dazed, through the sunny streets. They reached a tree-shaded lane, the houses on each side surrounded by lawns and flowering trees, and every garden protected by high fences and locked gates. It was quiet and cool there after the noise of the city, and deserted, and they could hear birds singing.

Mugo asked an old gardener for the house of He-who-whistles, but when they reached it the gate was shut and when Mugo tried to open it two huge dogs came rushing out, barking. Mugo and his uncle stepped back hastily, but a servant came to the gate, peering through the bars at them.

"Get away from here or I'll call the police."

Joshua stepped back silently, merging into the bushes, but Mugo spoke. "Please don't do that," he begged. "I am only a boy looking for the house of He-who-whistles."

"You have found it. What about it?"

"I have come to visit my aunt who works for He-who-whistles. She is known as She-who-has-bow-legs."

"She is your aunt? She is a bad woman. My master has sent her away. And you had better go away quickly as well."

He turned away from Mugo.

"But please—where has she gone?"

"How should I know? Where bad women go!"

He walked towards the house and Mugo, suddenly angry, shouted after him, "You are a liar! She is a good woman! Her father was a famous doctor … " But the man took no notice of that.

"You get away or I get police!"

"My aunt is a good woman! What can have happened?"

wondered Mugo. This was a very strange city and a strange country just now, he thought. Joshua stood quite still, almost part of the bushes. The lane was quiet and deserted. What were they to do now?

"Hey!"

The voice seemed to come out of nowhere.

"Hey! Behind you!"

From the wire fence of the next door garden a woman was smiling at him, a woman in a flowered headscarf with a round, gleaming face.

"You looking for your aunt? I heard you asking. You travelled long way to see her?"

"We have. But she's gone ... "

"Take no notice of what he says—she was a good woman. But they took against her here. They said she had a relative in the forest and they couldn't trust her."

"She was a good woman," said Mugo. "I'll just have to tell my father I couldn't find her ... "

"But I know where she is—she told me she'd found a room in the east part of the city. Very poor place near the market, but it was shelter for her and her children ... "


It was as they reached the main road again that Mugo caught a glimpse of a police lorry and some policemen and heard the babble of voices. He turned swiftly to Joshua for advice, but Joshua had gone. Only a trembling branch in a thicket of bushes suggested where he might be. With no time to think, Mugo climbed into an empty dustbin at the gate of a house and pulled the lid on top. It was very cramped and hot in there, and smelt horrible. And he might have escaped, but fate intervened. The lid of the bin was lifted, and a shower of old banana leaves was dumped on to Mugo, who cried out and stood up. A woman shrieked, a policeman came running and Mugo found himself trying to explain what he had been doing in the dustbin. He tried to persuade them he was tired and wanted a rest, but they did not believe him, and he was pushed into a large caged lorry, which already had a handful of people in it, and rattled away into the city. Quite desperate, he stood clinging on to the cage and looking back towards the bush where he knew his uncle was hidden. Indeed, Mugo was an unlucky boy.

The men in the lorry did not speak much as they drove through the streets. They leaned against the wire netting, gazing out passively at the people in the streets, some of them smoking cigarettes. Mugo also looked out but he saw nothing. He did not know where he was being taken or what would happen. He was afraid that he would be put in prison and never see his family again. He was sure that Joshua would desert him now. What was there about Joshua that would make him care about what happened to Mugo? He was finished with Mugo now. He would take the opportunity to slip away, out of the city, to find his freedom in another land. Mugo was oppressed with fear and sadness and a great feeling of helplessness.

By the time they reached the police station, the lorry was filled with people who had not been able to satisfy the police that they had the necessary documents to prove who they were, and Mugo eventually found himself with the rest, standing in the compound of the police station, with half a dozen policemen pushing at them and shouting orders.

"What are they saying?" Mugo asked the man beside him.

"They are saying, 'Short people behind.'"

"Short people? I suppose that means me," said Mugo, preparing to go to the back of the crowd.

"They are also saying," said the man meaningfully, "'Tall people in front.'"

"Well, I am not tall, certainly," said Mugo.

"That does not depend on height," said the man. "That depends on the money in your pocket. Money in your pocket can make you a tall man."

Mugo was puzzled. He had money in his shirt pocket but he did not see how it could make him tall.

"That police inspector there—he is known as He-who-likes-tall-people. Always he will allow tall people to go in safety. If you have money, boy, go to the front, give him the money and you will be free."

Mugo found this difficult to believe, but he took his money out of his shirt pocket to count it. Less than fifteen shillings left. Hesitantly, he went forward to the front of the crowd and right up to the inspector himself. The crowd fell silent as they watched this young and ragged boy approaching the great man, He-who-likes-tall-people.

"Boy—what d'you think you're doing?" roared the policeman.

"Please, sir," said Mugo, "I think you like tall people, and I would like to be one. Will you take this?" And he handed over all the money he had.

For a moment there was a dreadful silence, while the policeman frowned at the money, and Mugo expected to be put in prison any moment. Then suddenly the man roared with laughter, put the money in his pocket and shouted, "Let this very tall person go free!"

There was a lot of noise from the crowd then, and Mugo

was escorted to the gate and pushed out into the street. He could hardly believe it, and he stood blinking in the sunshine, wondering what he could possibly do now with no money, no uncle, no aunt and in a strange town. His legs still trembling from his experience, his heart filled with panic at his own loneliness and helplessness, he began to wander aimlessly down the street, past the high walls of the police station. It was only when he had reached some shops that a hoarse, familiar voice said behind him, "You tick! Can you never learn? Why do you want to lead us into such danger?"

## 18

IT was with a feeling strange to him, something almost like gratitude and happiness, that Mugo found himself walking by Joshua's side. He had never imagined he would be happy to be with his uncle again.

Eagerly, Mugo explained what had happened to him.

Joshua glared at him.

"You mean you gave away all our money?"

"I had to. I had to be tall enough to get away. Would you rather I'd stayed in prison?"

"You might as well have done. You're no good to me if you've got no money. Here we are penniless ... "

"My aunt can help us."

"Let's find this aunt of yours ... "

It was Mugo who asked directions of the shopkeepers and stall-holders and market women, until they were directed to a shanty town in a hot, marshy valley near the edge of the city. Mugo's spirits sank as they walked among the houses that were made of mud or scrap-wood, or old packing-cases. The rainy season was beginning, and the rain of the night before had made the dirt roads into muddy tracks. It was close and fetid among the houses, which were ram-shackle and teeming with people. By asking and asking, Mugo and Joshua eventually reached a small mud house with an iron roof and a low doorway. In the dark, hot interior, they were directed to a door and it was opened to them by a small dark woman, quite clearly She-who-has-bow-legs, who was at first suspicious, and then wept with joy at seeing Mugo again. She-who-has-bow-legs had also two small babies who played on the mud floor of the room. There was only one small window, and the room was very hot. A few boxes seemed to serve as furniture, and some heaps of sacks and blankets as beds. It was another shock for Mugo. He had always been told that his aunt who worked in the city had a room of her own in the garden of her employer's house, and that it had a tap at the door and every luxury. Yet here she was living in indescribable poverty.

With the tears running down her face she drew him into the room crying out that she was happy to see someone from the village again. It had been so long since she had had any news, and had he travelled so far alone? Then she saw Joshua.

"Who is this with you?"

"It's my father's brother, Joshua. Don't you remember him, Aunt? He's travelling with me."

His aunt backed away from them, drawing her children to her and shaking her head.

"Why have you brought him to my house? Do you want to bring misfortune to me and my children? Haven't we suffered enough through him?"

Joshua came no further into the room.

"I can go again."

"No, no, Uncle. We have to rest for a time. We have to make plans … " insisted Mugo. "Please, Aunt. For a little while … "

She-who-has-bow-legs sulkily shut the door behind them and they stood there awkwardly in the tiny room.

"Did anyone see you come here? You don't know what danger we live in from the police and from the friends of the forest fighters—and you bring him here—him, the known enemy of Mwengo! He lost me my job—he's been responsible for all my misery!"

Joshua only glared at her once, and then sat down on the floor, slumping against the wall.

"Tell her what we want," he said to Mugo.

"Does your father know you are here? With him?"

Mugo nodded.

"He must be mad! The whole family must have gone mad!"

"We are travelling to Mombasa, Aunt. He's getting a ship there and leaving the country. It's the only way. But we need money ... and food ... "

"Money! Ooi! I've no money! If he's a relative of yours, don't think you have money! Or peace of mind!" Joshua only looked at her and away. "He was a great talker! Always! The things he promised us!"

She-who-has-bow-legs cried noisily again, then she stopped. "Well, at least you must eat something. The food is poor enough, but eat it and welcome."

But Joshua would not touch it.

She-who-has-bow-legs only tightened her lips. Mugo thought he should refuse the food also, but he was hungry, and his aunt insisted that he ate.

"As for the train fare to Mombasa!" She threw up her hands. "I have no money and no means of getting it. But I'll go out and try to get you a better shirt and a pair of trousers that aren't torn. And I'll see what news is about."

Nervously, she picked up the two children and left the house.

All the fight and cunning seemed to have gone out of Joshua. He sat on the floor, his back against the wall, his long coat in folds about his bent knees, his head drooping. It had begun to rain, and the drumming sound on the roof drowned the noise from outside. And water dripped through a hole in the ceiling, gradually forming a pool by Joshua's still figure.

Mugo sat on the floor also and at intervals looked across at Joshua. He couldn't believe his uncle had no plan for them, no cunning idea that would get them to Mombasa. He seemed sunk into a final despair. So they sat in the room saying nothing, with the drumming rain filling their ears, and Mugo himself began to think desperately of what they might do.

His aunt came in suddenly, pulling a cloth from her head and shaking rain from it on to the floor, her face glistening with water and her black eyes rolling white with fear.

"You will have to go now," she said.

Joshua looked up. A stern look came over his face, and he stood up slowly, with a certain dignity.

"You do not have to worry, *woman*!"

"You don't understand—listen!"

Drowning the sound of the rain they heard a distant murmur and muttering, as though a river were in flood.

"What is it?" asked Mugo.

"It is all Nairobi—they are looking for you, Joshua! If they find you, they will tear you apart! Before they get here, *go* …"

Joshua buttoned up his long coat. As Mugo watched, he pulled his dark glasses from his pocket and was about to put them on, then hesitated and thrust them back in his pocket.

"They will be looking for a blind man," he said, almost to himself. He looked round, in a dazed way as though he didn't know any longer where he was, and Mugo jumped up and went to him.

"I'm coming with you."

"Stay here, boy."

"We go together to Mombasa."

Joshua shook his head.

"They will be looking for a man and a boy."

"I will not walk with you, but behind you. I can look out for danger also."

But the door of the shanty had already swung shut behind Joshua.

"You stay with me, Mugo," his aunt was saying. "It is too dangerous out there ... "

Mugo shook his head. For the first time he felt pity for Joshua, the pity one feels for an animal that has been a proud and fierce creature and that is now at bay.

"He needs me," said Mugo. He hastily opened up his bundle, and hardly noticed his aunt's cry of alarm at the sight of the gun which he thrust into the belt of his trousers. He pulled the blanket over his head and prepared to leave.

His aunt pushed a bundle of white nylon into his hand. "Here—a clean shirt, at least. Be careful, Mugo! Go well!"

Mugo stepped out after Joshua into the mud path of shanty town.

The distant growl became a sudden overwhelming roar, and Mugo caught a glimpse of Joshua stepping back quickly between two huts as a shouting crowd flooded round a corner, filling the alley. Mugo also stepped back, clinging to a window-sill to avoid being swept along in the crowd that shouted as they went, "Kill Joshua! Kill the traitor!"

Banners bounced and sailed over the surface of the crowd. On one was a huge picture of Mwengo, dead, lying with staring eyes, his gun at his side. Following it came a banner with the same picture, but the body had Joshua's face not Mwengo's. "Kill Joshua — traitor!" said the words beneath.

When the procession had finally passed, the alley was silent with a kind of exhaustion. One or two women crept to their doors to look out, some children cried. The crowd still howled in the distance. Mugo saw Joshua appear again from between the houses, and, trembling from fear of that crowd, Mugo followed him.

It was clear that Joshua did not know where to go. They went through the narrow lanes between the market stalls and passed the wayside barbers, passed a street full of small garages and then on to the wide streets, where cars swooped through the rain and shoppers sheltered in doorways. Wet and chilled and worried, Mugo plodded on, never letting Joshua out of sight.

There was a distant wailing of a siren that at first meant nothing to Mugo until it came closer and closer, and deafened and frightened him. It was a police car, gliding along to the end of the road where it stopped, blocking the traffic. Joshua had seen it, and he turned, and together they began running in the opposite direction. But there was the mutter and shouts of the crowd again, and the procession with its banners crossed at the end of the street. "Kill Joshua! Kill the traitor!" came the chant.

They stopped, flattened against the wall, as the policemen came running towards them, rounding up all the men and boys as they went. And among them, Mugo suddenly saw the thin features of the Homeguard, looking, looking, searching with a determined eye among the crowds.

They stood between the advancing police and the mob. There was no escape. Joshua must be recognized.

Mugo twisted round as a hand grasped his arm.

"Don't stay on the streets, man," a deep voice said, "they're picking up every African they can find. You strangers here?"

Mugo nodded into the dark, kindly face.

"Keep close to me, then … "

They followed the stranger through back streets and lanes which he seemed to know well, to a small truck in a car park. The police sirens and the chanting of the crowd were distant and faint.

The stranger pulled the tarpaulin cover from the back of the truck and put the big box and the carrier bag he was carrying into the truck.

"You got kipande?" he asked, grinning. "Special pass—you got one?"

Joshua grunted. "We've *no* passes. This is the road to Mombasa?"

"It is. But there'll be police checks all round the city. Look, if you want to get to Mombasa, you and the boy, get under the tarpaulin. You can rely on me to get you to Umoja—from there it'll be easy."

They did not speak as the truck bumped its way out of the city and on to the long road to Mombasa. It was dark and hot under the tarpaulin, but it was safe. After they reached Umoja—well, there might be danger again, but he would think of that later. In the meantime, Mugo slept.

The Umoja Friends Bar was a shack by the roadside and was run by the man who had brought them from Nairobi. He gave them cool beer to drink and told them they had 199 miles yet to go. They sat in the shade of his bar looking

K

out at the hot stretch of road, the bare, rusty landscape and the large elephant, red from the earth, that stood on the verge of the road opposite. After a while it turned its back on them ponderously and walked away in the direction of the middle of Africa.

Mugo thought of the many miles they had yet to walk, and his heart sank at the thought of it. They were out of Nairobi, but it was certain that word would be sent ahead to the police to look out for them in Mombasa.

"Thank you for your help, man," said Joshua as they got ready to leave. "You saved us from many difficulties. Stay well … "

"Not so fast, man," said the owner of the bar. "You can't walk all that way. You better wait for the train."

And he told them that behind the bar was Umoja station and the train from Nairobi that evening would stop there for water, and that his friend was a guard who would certainly turn a blind eye if they wanted to hop on a goods truck—he was a thoughtful and generous man, the first they had met with in six days on the run.

And so, in the dark warmth of the night, amid the wind and the strange cries of the African plain, Mugo hid with Joshua behind a bush and listened while the earth trembled with the approach of the iron serpent. And he trembled himself as he followed Joshua across the platform and swung into a truck and the serpent shrieked its defiance at the black African sky and shuddered, and moved faster and faster towards Mombasa.

## 19

THEY had reached Mombasa—they had reached the sea. They had come to the very edge of their land, and the end of the journey was near.

Fort Jesus, a grim old fortress built by the Portuguese, looked out from the coast of Mombasa to the glitter of the Indian Ocean, its grey, precipice-like walls rising from a narrow strip of grass and trees beside the water. Mugo and his uncle sat under the shadow of the trees and watched the wide sails of an Arab dhow leaning against the sky as it approached the old harbour.

"If we could get you on to a ship like that," said Mugo. They had travelled in the iron serpent all night, and got out at Mombasa station in the cool sunny morning to another strange world of Arabs and Indians and few, so far as Mugo could see, of his own people. It was a white Arab town with clustering palm trees and a warm damp wind off the sea blowing the rubbish about its narrow streets and strangely shaped mosques. They had begged a drink of water, but had had no food, and no money for any, and so they had made their way down to the sea where they could at least watch the ships that might take Joshua to safety.

Joshua said nothing. His eyes narrowed as he watched the dhow, and Mugo felt a twinge of uncertainty. It seemed an impossible distance between his uncle and that ship.

"Perhaps," said Mugo, "if I could find the Arab merchant my father spoke about he would give us some food. And also, he might lend the money for your trip to Egypt. My father would pay him back."

A sneer spread over Joshua's face. "Oh yes. Just as your father said. You remember that nice straight road from the village to Mombasa that he had planned for us—you remember how nice and straight it was."

"It was you made it crooked—you didn't tell my father everything."

"Everything! I couldn't foresee everything!"

There was a bitter silence.

Joshua grunted. His shoulders hunched as he watched the dhow slide round the headland towards the Old Harbour.

"So, what do we do?"

Mugo went back into the town alone. It had been his idea that it would be safer if Joshua stayed away from the busy streets in case he was recognized. And Mugo intended to find Sheikh Ali Mohammed.

It was two days before Christmas, and the streets of the town were busy, but the distant howl of motorbikes brought hesitation to the people, and police outriders appeared, making cars pull in to the curb, forcing pedestrians back to the pavement. In the crowd, Mugo stood and watched while a big car went slowly by with a white man sitting in it, followed by more cars and more police.

"Who is that?" he asked the man next to him.

"The District Officer for this area. There must be trouble —look at all the police!"

The Jeep that brought up the procession confirmed Mugo's suspicions as to what the trouble was. In the back of the Jeep rode the Homeguard, looking now lonely and isolated and very stern. The search for Joshua had reached Mombasa.

He found Salim Road and went into the Old Town, along the narrow streets with their high, blank walls of houses on either side, here and there a grilled window, or the open doorway to a dark cavernous warehouse. Mugo went nervously. The canyon-like streets oppressed him, for he was used to the low, crouching huts on the wide plains. There were so many foreign people—so many Arabs and Indians in their strange dresses. To him they had a sinister air. He halted beside the large white building which could, he thought, be the Jain Temple, but he was afraid even to approach anyone to ask about Sheikh Ali.

A group of small Arab boys in long white robes stood giggling at his flat nose, frizzy hair and torn clothes as he hesitated at a junction of two lanes. Looking round nervously he caught a glimpse of a face that watched him from a slit of window and then moved out of sight. Mugo had never been in such a place before. His mouth was dry with fear, and he was on the point of turning and running back to the fort when he saw the faded white lettering above an old and crumbling warehouse—Sheikh Ali Mohammed, Carpets.

Mugo went cautiously to the open door and peered in. At first he could make out nothing in the dimness, and then he started back as he realized that someone was sitting in there watching him.

"Come here, boy," said a commanding voice.

Mugo went slowly inside, gradually making out a figure

in a long white robe and a ragged beard seated at a desk. He was drinking coffee from a small white cup, and a ring sparkled on his finger as he raised his hand to wipe his beard. He was very thin and very old, and his eyes stared sharply and brightly at Mugo.

"Come here."

Mugo went slowly into the dimness, over the warm wooden floor, and stopped beside the desk. The room was very close and filled with a strong reek of carpets and fermenting dates.

"Are you a thief?"

Mugo hastily shook his head.

"Are you Sheikh Ali?"

"That is my name."

"I am Mugo, son of Wamba."

"A bara boy, eh? From up-country? A village boy." Sheikh Ali sipped more coffee. "What are you doing in Mombasa?"

Mugo was disappointed. He felt sure Sheikh Ali would have remembered his father's name.

"My father was Wamba. Son of Mugo," he said earnestly.

The bright eyes searched his face. The smell of dates was overpowering.

"Wamba, son of Mugo?"

"Yes."

"I once knew a Wamba. Though I cannot remember whether he was son of Mugo."

"He was." Mugo was eager. "He was your sweeper. You had just set up your warehouse."

"I had come from Egypt. I was younger then. I had brought carpets here in one of my father's dhows, and I found this warehouse empty and rented it. I needed a sweeper, and this bara man came peering round the door, just as you did, asking for work. He had just returned home after serving in the British Army during the war. He had a bullet hole in his leg."

"He has still," said Mugo proudly. "And my grandfather, Mugo, son of Wamba, still wears my father's greatcoat from the army."

Sheikh Ali's face broke into a wide smile that sent the wrinkles running over his face. "You are that Mugo? Then you are welcome. Come, sit down." He pointed to a stool and poured out coffee which Mugo drank thankfully.

Sheikh Ali stroked his beard. "You are alone?"

Mugo nodded.

"You are a long way from your home."

Mugo nodded.

For some time they sat in silence. The coffee flowed into Mugo's empty stomach, and he began to feel happier and less overcome by the smell of dates.

"My father sent me to you. He said I should seek your help."

"Any help I can give will be given."

He poured more coffee, and Mugo drank it.

"I have a relative who is in trouble. He must leave the country and go to Egypt. But I have no money to pay his fare and I know no captains of ships."

Sheikh Ali looked at Mugo sidelong from his long, dark eyes. He sipped more coffee and then he laughed.

"You are certainly in need of help, Mugo son of Wamba." Then he stopped smiling. "This relative, is he a forest fighter?"

"He has given up all that," said Mugo earnestly.

"Do you think they can?"

Mugo thought suddenly of his uncle's bitter look out to sea, and his thoughts of not going to Egypt, and his trickiness in the forest. And he doubted.

"I cannot say truthfully that he has given it up. But he will have to give it up, you see."

"Mugo," said the old man, who spoke like this because of a whim, "I will help this man. But he must not come here. You understand. It would be a danger to me, and besides, I do not trust him," and he laid his hand on the hilt of his dagger and looked sternly out on to the narrow patch of sunlit street. For a few moments he thought and then said, "Tomorrow, on the early tide, one of my ships sails. She is the *Kima* and her captain is Jahiz. See that this relative of yours is down at the Old Harbour at sunrise and the captain will be expecting him as a deck passenger. There will be no questions. But tell him to be careful—and be quiet."

"I cannot—cannot thank you ... " Mugo felt suddenly very weary and exhausted. Was the long journey over?

"There is no need, Mugo son of Wamba. But, you need a bath—your smell is not that of jasmine!—and some food, and some clean clothes. Come, Mugo ... "

Two hours later, in the hot stillness of the afternoon when not a breath of air stirred the dust in the corners of the Old Town, Mugo left Sheikh Ali's warehouse and went with a jaunty step towards the fort. He was clean, he had eaten and he wore a new pair of trousers and a shirt. He had good news for his uncle and the money for his train journey back to his village in his pocket. Ngai, and Sheikh Ali, had been very good to him. As he went a song of happiness broke from his lips and he danced to its tune out of the Old Town:

Who was it helped Mugo, son of Wamba,
When he was in need?
Weey-ii, Weey-ii.
Sheikh Ali, his father's friend,
He came to the help of Mugo.
He will always be remembered—
Weey-ii, Weey-ii ...

And then the song died on his lips, a hand caught at his shoulder and twisted him into a corner, and he looked up into the angry face of the Homeguard.

"So—I have found you, you little traitor!"

One thing Mugo was determined not to do was to betray Joshua. They could do what they liked—they could torture him, they could kill him. He would not betray.

"Where is he? Where is that evil man who was responsible for the death of C.I. Mackenzie?"

"He did not mean the C.I. to die," stammered Mugo.

"He led us into a trap."

"He meant only Mwengo to die. And me perhaps. Not the C.I. The C.I. had promised him money!"

"You are lying!"

"It is the truth!"

The Homeguard pushed Mugo against the wall and stood back from him. His rifle was still on his shoulder, and Mugo looked down, half expecting his shoe to be still gaping, but he was wearing new boots with a high shine.

"I have promised," he said, "I have sworn to avenge the C.I.'s death! He was my Higher Up."

"I did not kill him."

"You know where his killer is!"

"I can't tell you!"

"You are stubborn like all your family!"

"Like my beautiful sister!"

The Homeguard's face softened. He smiled. "Look, boy," he said. "That uncle of yours. He has brought nothing but trouble to your family. That is so?"

Mugo nodded. It was true.

"He is wicked and untrustworthy. I have sworn to capture him for the sake of the C.I. But you, Mugo. Think of it. You could bring a criminal to justice, you could release your family from the shame and trouble he has brought. And more—you could take riches back to your father. Think of it, Mugo. Think of the reward on Joshua's head. Help me to capture him, and we share the reward! Think of the goats your father could buy for you!"

Mugo thought of it. It was true. So much money would make him a rich man all his life. And he thought of Joshua and the trouble he had brought his family. And he thought of how Joshua had tried to abandon him, and sent him into an ambush and then run off. There was nothing very good to be said of Joshua. But then, Joshua had been in a difficult position. He had fled from Mwengo and been captured by C.I. Mackenzie. He had been between them both, and maybe the trap he arranged had been a just one. He had brought together both his enemies in the forest—and had they not been seeking each other anyway? As for himself, Mugo could forgive Joshua, and he must anyway follow out his father's wishes. He must get Joshua on a ship.

Mugo looked up at the Homeguard. He looked as innocent as he could.

"Joshua is heavily armed. He will not be taken easily," he said.

"*I* will take him!"

"No, no," said Mugo. "Listen. I will bring him to a place where you can take him. Only you must promise me half the money."

"It is promised."

"And you must not follow me. That would end everything."

"It is promised."

"Where shall I bring him?"

"The police station would be best. This evening before dark. Just walk past. We will be waiting."

# 20

"I'VE arranged everything with Sheikh Ali."

Mugo sat down under the tree beside his uncle Joshua and looked out to sea. In the cool of the day many of the towns-people had come to walk there, and they wandered past the forest fighter, unknowing.

"There are too many people," muttered Joshua, his eyes rolling uneasily.

"The plan is very simple," said Mugo.

Joshua said nothing.

"You must go."

Still he said nothing.

"The Homeguard is in Mombasa. He has sworn to avenge C.I. Mackenzie."

Joshua spat. "That hyena! That rhino."

"Uncle Joshua, you *must* go," pleaded Mugo.

Joshua shrugged.

"I will go," he said.

They spent the night huddled beneath the trees under the old fort. A moon shone frostily over the sea, and a cool wind whispered through the plane trees and chilled them. Twice Mugo wakened and was aware of his uncle sitting staring out to the sea, still, like a carved mask.

It was Joshua who finally wakened him as daylight was

breaking, and they gathered up what possessions they had and went cautiously into the streets.

They were surprisingly busy even then, for it was the day before Christmas and the traders wanted to do as much business as they could. Besides, there was a big ship full of European tourists in harbour.

Mugo and Joshua walked down the road towards the Old Harbour, very conscious of their danger in that street where there were no crowds to hide them.

From behind them they heard, suddenly, the sound of voices singing, and the deep beat of a drum and the high tinkle of a tambourine and the sound of a trombone. They turned and saw a group of children and adults, rejoicing that it was Christmas, coming towards them, dancing and playing and singing a Christmas hymn and begging money for their church. They danced joyfully along the pavement towards Joshua and Mugo. But turning round again Mugo saw the Homeguard, standing hesitantly at the edge of the pavement, looking along the street. He did not need to tell Joshua, for Joshua was already among the crowd of dancers. He had seized a tambourine and was beating it and dancing and singing, and holding it up before his face. The dancers didn't seem to notice. They swept towards Mugo, and he joined them quickly, waving his handkerchief before him and keeping behind the crowd. The Homeguard watched in puzzlement something which was quite new to him as the crowd danced past, then turned away again to scan the street.

Joshua and Mugo danced on towards the Old Harbour.

There was a lot of activity round the *Kima* as the ship was got ready for sea, and on the jetty a small group of people stood shouting and gesticulating round her captain. Joshua and Mugo watched them from a distance.

"Is something the matter?" asked Mugo doubtfully.

"They will only be quarrelling about the fare." Joshua turned away to look back to the west over his homeland. Was he regretting having to leave, Mugo wondered? Or did the evil in his blood make that kind of feeling impossible for him? He had come a long way, down a steep hill, that young man who had made the speech about freedom.

Joshua stood with his head thrown back defiantly, his face stern. I can go home, Mugo thought. He can only go among strangers for the rest of his life. He was filled with sadness for the exile at this unhappy parting. What could he say?

"Go well, Uncle Joshua."

"Stay well, Mugo." Joshua spoke ironically, and looked back over his shoulder. A Jeep in the distance was moving slowly along the edge of the harbour towards them.

"Is it the Homeguard?" he asked.

Mugo strained his eyes to see. He went forward a few yards. He couldn't be sure. When he turned again, Joshua had gone. He was speaking to the captain, and in a moment had joined the stream of passengers walking on board, still limping, his coat still flapping around him.

Joshua had not looked back. Mugo had stood for a long time, watching Joshua find a place on the deck of the dhow, standing beneath the shadow of her sails, and looking out to sea. He had heard the captain's orders, watched the ship move away from the jetty into the morning sunlight. Joshua looked round then. He did not wave. Mugo's eyes misted, as he watched the dhow leaving.

"Goodbye, Uncle Joshua," he murmured to himself. "If

I am not the same Mugo who left the village eight days ago, it is because of you that I am different."

Well, he thought, pleased with his success, he would hurry to the old fort and watch the dhow leave harbour. Then he would go to the railway station to wait for the train back to Nairobi. What stories he would have to tell the boys in the village when he got home!

He stooped to pick up his bundle ...

It wasn't there!

It had been at his feet a little while ago—before Joshua left.

Filled with anger he raised his fist and shook it at the slowly moving dhow. The bundle with the Decider in it and his money for the journey home was in the dhow with Joshua. Success! He sneered at himself. He hadn't even learnt not to trust Joshua, not to pity him, because Joshua would always return evil for good! He would always be one jump ahead! If I get home, thought Mugo, I'll tell nobody of this last foolishness—only my father. Perhaps he will understand.

A sharp, explosive crack just behind his head made him drop to the ground with all the new instinctiveness he had learnt from Joshua. He recognized at once the smell of gunfire in his nostrils, and at the same moment he had a clear glimpse of a man's figure on the dhow also falling to the deck.

Mugo twisted round and looked up at the bare knees, the sharply pressed shorts, the long nose of the Homeguard, just lowering his rifle with a nod of satisfaction.

"I've done my duty—diligently *and* scientifically," he said, and looked down sternly at Mugo. "I've avenged the death of C.I. Mackenzie and I've killed the snake in the old hut."

159

Mugo stood up, feeling his knees tremble, and looked anxiously out at the dhow, and then back at the stern and satisfied features of the Homeguard. Was he right? Was it Joshua who had fallen there on the deck of the dhow, and had he been shot? The sun dazzled on the sea, the dhow lurched suddenly, her sails billowing. Mugo could not be sure. A man out there had fallen, and he had not risen again. But then could a man of Joshua's cunning be slain? Might he not just have dropped, instinctively like Mugo, at the threat of danger? Mugo realized he would never know. He would never know whether Joshua had died there and been buried at sea or lived to thrive in the narrow streets of some Egyptian town.

Without a further word, the Homeguard turned and marched back towards his Jeep, and with a final look at the dhow, Mugo turned and followed him, and the strengthening rays of the morning sun cast their long, dark shadows before them, and glanced off the barrel of the Homeguard's rifle. As for Mugo, he carried nothing now.